W9-DEW-828

Fox Tales

Oliver C.P. Armitage

© Copyright 1998 Oliver C.P. Armitage
All rights reserved. No part of this publication may be reproduced in any form without written permission from the author.

This book is a work of fiction. Names, characters, places, organizations and incidents are products of the author's imagination and are used ficticiously. Any resemblance to actual events, organizations, or persons, living or dead, is purely coincidental.

Library of Congress Catalog Card Number: 98-88357

ISBN 0-9667989-0-2

Printed by Sharp Printing
3477 Lockport Road
Sanborn, New York 14132

To those with fond memories of
Pennsylvania Military College
and Chester, Pennsylvania.

Acknowledgments

To those who assisted in creating this novel, please accept my sincere thanks, especially Gloria and Cindy for editing, Mimi for ideas and support, Jack Downes for reference material, Clarence Moll for reference and copyright counsel, Kate McCullough who never complained about the manuscript headaches, Brent Whitig for computer assistance, Bud Buckley for reference material, Les Jenkins for reference material and George Rathacker for his book cover graphics.

A Chester Brief

If William Penn found it a worthy spot to set foot, and General Washington found it able to accommodate his war-weary bones, it's appropriate to offer a few comments about old Chester where much of this novel finds itself.

Today the City has been milked of its sustenance. It's tired and hurting, suffering from economic erosion, too much public housing and political greed. But what a town it was: sitting in Pennsylvania on the huge Delaware River, beckoning industry and business to settle in its bounds.

Irving and Arasapha responded by opening mills; Roach opened his shipyard. The rest is history - The Pews with Sun Ship, Scott with Scott Paper, Ford with an assembly plant, then Atlantic Steel, Penn Steel and Baldt Anchor.

In those flapper and pre-World War II days, you could find a bit of everything. The choice of eight movie theaters, one being the grand Stanley Theater featuring the likes of the "Thundering Herd" of Woody Herman on Saturday nights. Stroll into a Sears, Montgomery Ward or Woolworth, buy a dress at Speares, a shirt at McCoy's or open a savings account in the Iron Workers Building and Loan. One might eat a delicious roast chicken dinner at the Yellow Bowl, drink a birch beer at Birney's, enjoy the cuisine and libation at the Washington House. On Saturday mornings, I remember the shoppers at Commission Row looking for fresh fish and vegetables. On Saturday night at the famous Bethel Court area, the "Ladies of the Night" offered their talents.

The fiber of the City was its generous ethnic mix, rich to poor - all endowed with pride. Many of the poor were immigrants. They labored at back breaking jobs providing strong family homes where education and character were paramount. These families were usually poor for only one generation: their children became business people, teachers, skilled laborers, lawyers and doctors - citizens of substance.

The City also boasted the second oldest military school in the country. Its demise and my affection for it prompted the influence of Pennsylvania Military College (now Widener University) in the Tales. Founded in 1821, P.M.C. was a small, private school, producing a proud, close knit alumni, who attained honors in both the military and private sectors. A surprising development occurred when polo became a major sport in the Twenties, Thirties and Forties. Just as surprising were the Indoor National Collegiate Championships they won, beating teams from Yale, Princeton, Harvard and Army. Polo always interested me and that led to writing a portion of the story to fit the polo scenario at the college. Some names that made polo what it was in that era include Wyman, Schaubel, Carroll, Hickman, Spurrier and Maloney.

Waterville Military Academy is the fictional college, A/K/A WMA, in the novel.

Chapter I

Chester's 5th Ward had bragging rights as the roughest, toughest neighborhood in the City limits. In the 1860's, Julia Fox was conceived and born in the 5th Ward.

Her father Jocko Fox was a hard drinking Irishman with black curly hair and smiling blue eyes. A chubby bundle of joy, her mother was Maureen Leahy, before she spotted Jocko. He had no chance once she made up her mind. Their blissful union resulted in their pretty little girl Julia.

Jocko Fox had had his usual stout at the East Ender. As he left the tavern feeling no pain, two overgrown thugs eyed him, hoping to bum half a buck or so for a couple of beers. The bigger of the two came up, looked him right in the eye and said, "How about four bits so's we can get a beer, Mate?"

Jocko smiled, "Sorry lads, I'm broke."

The big fellow looked him over carefully, thinking he might be an easy mark. "Come on, don't kid us, we could easily whip ya and take your money."

Jocko smiled again, "I wouldn't try it!"

With that, the smaller fellow threw a round house right which Jocko ducked. He returned the favor with an upper cut from downunder, catching the thug square on the chin, sending him sprawling. The big fellow launched his best shot from the blind side landing on Jocko's ear, dropping him to his knees. Jocko shook his head, jumped up and finished off the big fellow with a series of booming rights and lefts, depositing him in a trash can, rear end first. Jocko brushed himself off, lit up a cigar and proceeded on home. When he arrived, he quietly went to the living room and sat down in his stuffed chair. Maureen called him to dinner. When he didn't answer, she went to look for him and found him asleep in his chair. She gave him a shake, he never answered, his head fell forward. He died of a massive heart attack.

Julia was a victim of her father's early demise. Her mother brought home very little money from her job as a domestic, and as a result, Julia barely finished eighth grade before she quit school. She found work in the old Yellow Bowl restaurant washing dishes six nights a week.

As she turned eighteen, she worked laboriously, finally becoming a waitress. Working long hours with stingy tips made her look forward to Sunday: her day off.

Julia worked her fool head off late in the month of June. The weather was prematurely hot, and during Mass, she day dreamed about a swim in Ridley Creek. Sunday turned out to be a beautiful day. After Mass, she hurried home, found her bloomered swim suit in the storage trunk in the basement and tried it on. Julia had grown making the suit a tight fit. Also she'd developed in all the right places. Posing in front of the bureau mirror, she realized the swim suit hid most of her figure. After telling her mother of her plans, she slipped her dress on over her bathing suit and set out for the swimming hole, close to where the creek met the Delaware River.

At the swimming hole, a large dead tree angled out over the creek. It served two purposes: swimmers dove from it, and they swung from a rope attached to a high limb out into the middle of the creek then dropped with a great splash.

Julia was coaxed to try the rope by a friend. She reluctantly agreed, putting the rope over her shoulder as she carefully climbed the tree to the jumping point. Second thoughts were brought on by nervousness and the uncertainty of not having tried it before. Her swimming left something to be desired: she only knew the side stroke. As she thought about climbing back down, the other swimmers shouted words of encouragement. Holding the rope in both hands, she looked down at the creek. All of a sudden, she took the leap and swung through the air. She sort of panicked, gripping the rope tighter. Instead of dropping at the top of the arc, she held on and started to swing back. She didn't want to let go. Swinging all the way back, she smacked into the tree and hit her head. Dazed, she lost her grip and fell into the water going under. She surfaced still groggy and in trouble.

One of the swimmers, a tall young man sensed the problem. He dove into the creek and reached Julia quickly, pulling her over to the bank where he was able to stand. Suddenly, Julia became aware of the handsome young man helping her. Looking at him she said, "Thank you. I don't quite know what happened."

After they climbed the bank and were seated on the ground, he said, "You forgot to let go of the rope and swung back into the tree, dropping into the water. You were in trouble so I went in to give you a hand." He took her hand, "You were groggy, sort of out of it. Are you starting to feel better?" He let go of her hand and went to fetch her dress, then rolled it up to make a pillow, placing it on the ground. "Lie back and rest for a few minutes. It'll do you good."

She studied him thinking, what good looks, rugged, tall and lean. She asked, "Where you from, Chester, Eddystone?"

He looked directly at her, "I'm not from this area. Sort of passing through. However, I like it here, maybe I'll stay."

Several minutes passed and Julia sat up, "It'd be nice if you stayed, maybe we could swim another time. I'm Julia Fox." She waited a few seconds then asked, "Who are you?"

"Robert Shoemaker. My friends call me Lucky. I'm spending some time with my sister over in Leiperville. Think we could meet next Sunday?"

"I'd like that. How about 2:00 o'clock?"

During the week, Julia frequently thought about Lucky. She was smitten with his good looks and impressed with his quick thinking, heroic act. She eagerly looked forward to Sunday. The week passed painfully slow.

Lucky's sister knew nothing of the incident with Julia, and while he gave no indication of settling down, she hoped she could be a matchmaker. During the passing week, Lucky was introduced to a friend of his sister's - April. A large boisterous girl, she sang in the

Methodist Church choir as an off-key contralto. Many viewed her as an overly religious, innocent, young lady.

Lucky invited April for an evening stroll and a soda on Wednesday. While they were returning to April's home, she suddenly stopped and said, "Kiss me." Lucky quickly took advantage of the offer and discovered a very passionate companion. There was no convenient spot for him to take advantage of his surprising discovery and after a healthy exchange of some kissing and feeling, he escorted her to her door. She gave him a kiss and suggested another date. Lucky wasn't impressed with her loud booming tone, so he ducked a firm date, saying he was tied up the next few days but he would be in touch.

Lucky was constantly on the alert for a lascivious affair and while he was conscious of his date coming on Sunday, it was the least of his concerns for the next few days. He still had time to develop a new relationship or two. April was on hold until he determined if he could do better.

As things turned out, nothing developed. On Sunday he was waiting by the creek when Julia arrived with starry-eyed innocence. To him, she would be another easy conquest with no strings. On the other hand, she had thought about Lucky the entire week, waiting impatiently.

His plan was a quick one-timer. When he looked at her walking toward him, he realized what a striking find she was. Then and there Lucky decided he was going to have her, come hell or high water.

She had willed herself not to be frightened, but to seize every opportunity. Now that the time was nearing, she had that nervous feeling in the pit of her stomach.

Lucky approached her, reaching out to take her hand. "I'm glad you came. What's in the basket?"

"I packed some sandwiches, several cup cakes and some lemonade. Why don't we take a swim before we eat?"

"I'm getting hungry, but I'll take a quick dip if you like."

Julia went in first with Lucky diving in after. He came up and swam over to her. He thought, what a perfect time to steal a kiss. Little did he know, Julia was hoping he would.

When he put his arms around her and pulled her to him, she cooperated eagerly. What followed was an emotionally driven embrace with heated kissing and pelvic action: each responding to the passion of the moment.

Julia was very innocent, but totally infatuated with Lucky. She was determined to peak his interest so, putting aside her inhibitions, she let herself do what came naturally.

Lucky whispered in her ear, "Let's go find a secluded spot. We can eat and relax enjoying each other. I'd say we have a little unfinished business."

Julia gathered her picnic food together and they walked away from the other swimmers. One hundred yards or so up stream they found what they were looking for: a hidden retreat.

After they enjoyed the repast, Lucky stretched out and pulled Julia to him, wrapping his arms around her. Julia knew it was love at first sight and hoped he would embrace her. She looked directly in his eyes and when he kissed her again, she responded with passionate eagerness.

Lucky thought how fortunate he was. This was going to be easier than he expected so he might as well enjoy every moment.

Julia had led a very sheltered life with no experience in love making so she began to let him have his way. She didn't wish to lose him, but suddenly she caught herself. Slow down, you barely know him or how he feels toward you. She stiffened and pulled away.

Lucky sensed the problem. He shifted gears, "Julia, honey, I'm falling for you." Looking into her eyes for a moment then kissing her ear, he whispered, "I love you."

"Oh Lucky, I want to believe you, but we hardly know each other."

"Darlin', the saying goes, 'you'll know when you find your true love!' I've just found mine."

She wanted to believe him, but a second sense told her he was moving too fast. She took her arms from around his neck, "Lucky, why don't we slow down and get to know one another, then we could go on from there. I do like you tremendously and it could very easily turn into love."

"Julia, I told you I love you. With some loving we can strengthen our feelings for each other." With that said, he went to kiss her lips; she turned her cheek to him.

The turn of events irritated him. He was tightly wound and he was becoming unstrung. He grabbed her face so that she couldn't turn her head and forced a kiss. When she started to struggle, he slapped her in the face which brought tears. Her cheek burned, she worked her hand free to rub it.

Lucky told her, "Hold still, if you yell or resist I'll choke you." Then he put his hands around her neck giving it a good wringing to show her he meant business.

He tried to get her swim suit off but struggled getting nowhere. He then told her to take it off. She said she couldn't. He slapped her with such force she fell back from her sitting position and started sobbing. She took her suit off.

Lucky dropped his swim suit and jumped on top of her forcing her legs apart. He forced himself into her with no foreplay. She yelped at the pain, he smacked her again, then put his hand over her mouth.

Although it was over rather quickly, it seemed like an eternity to Julia.

Lucky got up, put his bathing suit back on and stomped away, saying over his shoulder, "Don't follow me. I never want to see you again."

Lucky went back to his sister's house, changed clothes and left town without a word.

Julia was dazed. Her face was swollen. She slowly got back into her swim suit. She couldn't stop sobbing, not only because of the physical hurt but also the mental anguish. She was crushed by Lucky's vile nature and the ultimate rape. As her senses returned, she stopped sobbing and sadness and depression turned to anger. She was indeed in a difficult position. There was no one in whom she could confide or talk to about being raped.

Julia decided a jump in the creek might cool her down, ease the throbbing of her cheeks and give her time to collect her thoughts. She stayed in the water for some time, floating, dunking, soaking her cheeks in the cool water. The stinging started to subside. Eventually, she pulled herself out of the creek and lay on the grass beside the picnic. As the anger welled in her, she pulled on her dress over her wet bathing suit, picked up her picnic basket and blanket and headed for home. She decided to put on dry clothes and somehow get revenge.

She would first learn where he was. She went to his sister's address which he had given her. When she got to the house, the tenants said, "We've never heard of Robert Shoemaker." The wrong street and house number, maybe Lieperville was a lie too. Julia asked around, but in that Lucky had been in the area such a short time, few people knew him. After a week, she gave up, figuring he was gone, not to return.

Two months later Julia knew she was pregnant.

Chapter II

Gerald Fox was born out of wedlock in 1892.

Julia now worked as a housekeeper for the wealthy Howell family in the City's First Ward, home of many of the more prosperous residents. A WMA graduate, Mr. Howell had his cadet uniform, saber and other mementos meticulously preserved. When Julia came home, after a long day of house cleaning and laundering, she sat with a cup of tea and retold her young son the various WMA tales Mr. Howell shared with her.

As Gerry became a young boy, he lacked parental supervision, particularly when he came home from school. He was afforded many opportunities to get into trouble with his friends, and he did. Fortunately, he limited the extent of the trouble. What limited guidance he got from his mother impressed him. When he resisted going further in the gang activities, he was ridiculed and ended up defending himself.

One afternoon after school, he joined his pals Bungy and Tata to break in and explore a vacant house off old Morton Avenue. The house tempted them many times before on their way home from school. They decided the rear door was the easiest to break in and be the least conspicuous. They finally split the door frame, after heaving and ramming. The door finally sprung open. Roaming through all the rooms and the cellar, they found nothing to take. They sat on the worn pine floor in the living room, and Bungy pulled a cigarette stub from his shirt pocket and lit it. They passed it around, puffing it until the tip was a solid red glow. They felt like big shots, except when they coughed and choked trying to inhale. Tata had seen some wood in the cellar and suggested they build a fire in the small living room fireplace. Gerry balked, thinking of what the consequences might be. Both boys urged him to join them, but he said, "No, I have to get home." They teased and ridiculed him about being a mama's boy. Finally, he had had enough. He went over to Tata and gave him a shove. Tata fell backward, but recovered quickly, putting up his fists emulating his favorite prize fighter. He danced around Gerry, jabbing and feinting. Gerry's hot temper welled up, and he charged into Tata, both fists and arms moving like pistons, first toward his head then to his body. He was a tough one and very self-confident; he completely beat the tar out of Tata who was supposed to be one of the rougher, tougher young lads in the Fifth Ward.

Gerry's reputation now preceded him, but he still got into scraps. He became street smart, realizing, the best way to command respect was to be tougher than the next guy.

As Gerry attended junior high school, he often wandered up to WMA to watch cavalry maneuvers. His being around the ponies and stables helped him to know some of the grooms. Because he was persistent and of a congenial nature, eventually he was permitted to help cool down and groom the horses. His affection for the horses was obvious to everyone and the care with which he groomed them eventually got the stable manager's attention. It wasn't long until he was allowed to exercise a horse now and again. This was the start of Gerry's great love affair with horses.

Chapter III

1907

Gerry felt his fortunes were rewarded when in homeroom, he was seated directly in front of Philimina Ginetti. Phil was the daughter of strict Italian immigrants, proprietors of an Italian food market. She was born with innate beauty: brown eyes, long lashes, wavy black hair, a maturing figure with long slender legs.

Gerry and Phil's mutual interest in each other was immediate. They were both good students, keeping very busy: Phil working after school and weekends in the family store, Gerry with an early morning paper route. After school they walked home together discussing school, friends and what the future might hold for them. She hoped to marry and raise a happy family; he hoped to somehow go to Waterville Military Academy, riding in the cavalry. In the closing month of the school year, their classmates arranged a picnic at Chester Park, well within walking distance. Gerry was going and Phil wanted to go but knew she faced a difficult time with her parents. They expected her to work on Saturdays, and in addition, they would not condone a mixed affair if they were not with her. At sixteen, with new feelings developing, they intended to keep her under their watchful eyes.

Phil loved and respected her parents but at times became irked at the strict restrictions imposed on her. She tried to reason with them, then argued that she would be home before dark and all her friends were permitted to go. After listening to all her pleas, they reluctantly gave in; however, her older brother Angelo was to escort her to and from the picnic. She felt this was a ridiculous proviso when all her friends were permitted to come and go independently.

Most ten-year-olds had more liberty. However, it was that or nothing. Unhappily, she agreed.

Actually, Phil and Angelo were very close, and travelling to and from the picnic together worked rather well. Her concern was she wanted to be alone with Gerry, especially on the way home. She had to wait and see if anything could be worked out.

On the way to the picnic, Angelo told Phil he was not staying but would return to walk her home at seven o'clock. She liked the idea and said she would look for him.

Phil met Gerry at the picnic and shared her picnic basket with him as planned. She brought fried chicken, pickles, rolls and apple pie. They spread the blanket Gerry brought and sat down to enjoy the lunch. Later, the games started. They got into a tug-of-war. Each side had five boys and five girls. Gerry and Phil were on the same team at the end of the rope. Their team thought Gerry would make a good anchor. The tug began with each side pulling then giving ground. There were grunts and groans as everyone strained. Gerry and Phil dug their heels in, doggedly yielding ground. To Gerry and Phil, it seemed they were doing all the pulling. The other team had the momentum going, the adrenaline pumping, the advantage swinging their way. Gerry felt his team slipping toward the center line marker. Finally, with one determined effort, the other team pulled Gerry's team over the line, winning the contest. Both teams collapsed. In the process, Gerry inadvertently fell on top of Phil. Both let out a grunt as they landed on the ground. In that they were both spent, neither made an effort to move. Actually, each enjoyed the position in which they found themselves. Their faces were inches from each other, without another thought, Gerry stole a quick kiss. Phil's reaction was a warm inner feeling accompanied by a blush.

From this brief affectionate encounter they had fallen into, they were both anxious to spend some private time together.

They picked themselves up, brushed themselves off and wandered down to the bottom of a park hill where Ridley Creek flowed. Some of the classmates were fishing for sunfish. They walked hand-in-hand along the picturesque bank of the creek until they came to the waterfall. The area at the falls was deserted except for them.

They found a grassy spot and sat down to enjoy the serenity. As Gerry draped his arm around Phil's shoulder, she turned and looked directly into his eyes. He kissed her again: this time more slowly with an impulsive hug, and she put her arms around Gerry's neck. When the innocent kiss ended, they were both out of breath, having held their breaths for the duration of the kiss. Loving what they had discovered, neither wanted to leave. However, it was time for Phil to meet Angelo. Respectfully, they left their love nest, picked up the blanket and picnic basket, and found Angelo. As Gerry and Phil said goodbye, he watched her and her brother head for home.

When Gerry arrived home, he discovered his mother feeling terribly weak. She became weaker as the hours went on. Gerry consulted his neighbor for advice and was told to call his doctor.

Julia told Gerry she had been to a Dr. McKormic over on Seventh Street once, and she would prefer him as her physician. The doctor made the house call. He told Julia that she had had heart failure and would require rest and medication. Julia gave up her job and got the prescribed rest, but her illness lingered. Their meager savings were depleting.

An excellent student, Gerry was doing well in school, but in order to make ends meet, he realized he would have to quit, and go to work. On his last day at school, he encountered Mr. Josep, his science teacher. Mr. Josep had taken an interest in him, realizing the potential the young man had. Gerry decided to reveal his decision to the interested mentor.

After learning Gerry's plan to quit school and why, Mr. Josep told Gerry of a friend who had an ice and coal business that needed help with customer deliveries. He told him coal delivery was very hard work, but if he was interested, he would call and arrange an appointment with Herbert Curl, the owner of Chester Ice and Coal Company. Gerry told Mr. Josep he appreciated his concern but would like to sleep on it. He would be in touch with his answer the next day.

Chapter IV

Phil faced an inquisition when she and Angelo arrived home. Her father and mother wanted to know everything she had done. In giving them the details, she mentioned some of her classmates who had participated in the tug-of-war, among them she included Gerry. The Ginettis were immediately wanting to know more about the young man. In discussing him briefly, she became somewhat flustered. Her parents got the message and became concerned that an interest was aroused in the two young people. Even with their precautionary measures, their very own innocent daughter had become interested in the young man.

They wanted information about him and his family. She knew very little. She told them they were just friends, their concerns were unwarranted. She told them he a was very bright, good student. Mr. Ginetti told her that under no condition was she to encourage him, and she was not to see him outside school.

Phil worried over her father's restrictive order. She advised Gerry. On the surface, he took it fairly well; inside, it hurt. He had a special feeling for her. Maybe it was love. He wasn't sure; he never felt this way before.

Their time together was limited to school in the beginning. Their attraction to each other was so strong, they began to steal time together outside the limits of the school. It wasn't easy, as they didn't want someone reporting back to the Ginettis.

Joy and happiness filled each of their hearts. The time passed swiftly and the events that ended Gerry's schooling occurred. He told Phil of his decision to quit school and explore a possible job opportunity. He explained the job details and how he came to hear about it. With his mother critically ill, she knew he had no other choice. This presented another problem in their relationship. Her love had developed to the point where she considered a lifetime together. He was handsome, intelligent and treated her tenderly even though he was rough and tough. With all this, her parents would never consider a non-Italian, particularly one who quit school. None of that for their little flower.

Gerry quit school and started his job, which meant they didn't see as much of each other. Wanting something they couldn't have made the two young lovers want it more.

Phil decided it was time to try again with her folks. She told them all about him, his fine qualities, and how he had to quit school and go to work to take care of his sick mother. She told them she loved him, and asked their permission for him to call on her and to meet them.

The answer was emphatically "No." He would never be able to provide for her. She was told she was not to see him. As a result, their moments together were so few it was difficult to have even a casual relationship.

Now that Phil was prohibited from seeing him, Gerry's love grew stronger than ever! The few rendezvous they arranged were extremely brief, usually in some remote spot where they would not be recognized. If they held hands and stole a kiss, it was considered a gift of heaven. As time passed, the restrictions under which their relationship existed became almost intolerable.

Gerry's mother was more and more dependent on him. Her condition required rest, and her activities became very limited. He pondered over how and where he and Phil would live if he was ever able to marry her. Under the present circumstances, they would most likely live at his home. Although always clean and orderly, it offered the bare minimum. The coal heater gave off excessive amounts of coal gas. The hot water was heated by a manual Rudd gas water heater, lit only when you needed hot water. The bath had a tub and toilet only. The kitchen sink was used for lighter body cleaning. There was a very limited electric service. And there were only two small bedrooms, a living room and kitchen. If they decided to live there, the circumstances would be trying, at best.

Chapter V

1911

Gerry, now nineteen, had been working for the Chester Ice and Coal Company for three years. There was business competition, but the company fought it off time and again. Mr. Curl not only owned and ran the company very well, but he was a pillar in the community. He was well known, as he sat on City Council, and was a founder and director of one of the first savings and loans that sprung up during those years. These associations served the community needs for savings and home financing. He was on the vestry at St. Peter's Church and had been an influencing force behind the building of the new high school. His customers knew him and felt secure in having him take care of their ice and coal deliveries.

These deliveries were made by horse and cart. Most times the deliveries required the ice to be placed in the ice box in the house or the rear shed. The delivery men were carefully selected for this reason. In addition, if they were polite and efficient, it helped the business.

The coal required customer contact as well. The basement access window to the coal bin had to be opened from the inside which was handled by the delivery men. The coal was then carried in coal bags from the cart and dumped through the basement window. When the delivery was complete, the window was closed and locked.

Mr. Curl realized Gerry was an exceptional worker. He learned quickly, worked till the job was done, used his creativity and was honest. He had Gerry come to the office on Saturday to learn more about the bookkeeping and customer relation operations. He wanted to develop Gerry's potential; perhaps take him under his wing.

Mark Terrill had worked his way up as Mr. Curl's assistant - responsible for all company operations not attended to by Mr. Curl. Being a suspicious person by nature, he took offense to this new move and what possible implications it could have on his position in the future.

Gerry's duties during the week included working in the ice house filling the various needs of user customers, company deliveries and a selective group of vendors who serviced areas not covered by company routes.

He also worked making deliveries of both ice and coal. The coal deliveries were extremely heavy, dirty work: lugging tons of coal in bags from the coal carts to the house. The ice deliveries were cleaner and deliveries were made more quickly. On occasions, a lonely housewife or widow would make suggestive innuendos. Gerry, being young and inexperienced in those matters, let the suggestions pass, undisturbed.

A year had passed and Gerry was learning rapidly as Mr. Curl had him working in the office three days a week. A natural worrier, Terrill felt Gerry was a threat to his position. Gerry, on the other hand, never gave Terrill's job a thought. He was content and surprised that Mr. Curl was giving him this opportunity.

The truth of the matter was Terrill had been diverting company funds to himself. The amounts were small, but the embezzlement had been going on for some time. The ice business afforded this opportunity for Terrill, and it went on and on unnoticed.

Eventually, Gerry's duties shifted from one responsibility to another. One in which he was presently involved was inventory control. The inventory included ice and coal, the ice being the object of the present audit.

The ice was made in 300 lb. blocks which cost the company 18¢. The wholesale price was 75¢ to the delivery wagon dealers. If broken down to 50 or 100 lb. blocks, the price equalled $1.50 retail to customer users.

Terrill worked early mornings and late evenings before and after other employees came and went. When he took care of customer users during these hours, he charged the users the retail rate but recorded the sales at the wholesale rate. The difference of 75¢ went into his pocket.

Before Gerry became involved in management training, Terrill oversaw the inventory control duties and was able to conveniently cover up his embezzlement activities. Furthermore, with Gerry just learning, Terrill was not concerned that he would be discovered.

Gerry studied the ice inventory, determining that the company ice sales averaged 600 blocks a week. The number of ice wagons was known, but the customer user use varied from week to week. There were no radical changes in the financial income imputable to the ice division of the company - all obvious things were apparently normal, leaving Terrill's covert activities undetected.

Terrill meanwhile was devising a plan to involve Gerry in a scheme where the results would end his auditing activities along with his job. Terrill had noticed a button that dropped from Gerry's sleeve lying on the floor of the office. He quickly grabbed it and placed it in his pocket. Finding the button was exactly what Terrill needed to make his plan work.

Terrill and Gerry had access to the cash box along with Mr. Curl. Terrill took an unauthorized fifty dollars from it. Implementing his plan, he dropped the button in the box. To his advantage, he was responsible for the cash count.

Mr. Curl had a need to change some larger bills. He naturally went to the cash box. When he opened it, he spotted the button. Wondering why it was there, he felt an urge to count the money. When he finished, he discovered the box was fifty dollars short.

In that Terrill was responsible for the reconciliation, Mr. Curl approached him with the problem and the button. Terrill then made his own count and confirmed the shortage. As far as the button was concerned, Terrill said he thought he had noticed one missing on Gerry's cuff.

Chapter VI

Could Mr. Curl have misjudged Gerry's character? He prided himself on his ability to judge people. It was possible he'd made a mistake. In any event, it was time to confront Gerry.

Gerry stood respectfully in front of Mr. Curl who was seated at his desk. Not aware of what the meeting was about, he expected questions regarding his audit of the ice business. He was surprised and dismayed when Mr. Curl opened the discussion with, "Gerry we're fifty dollars short in our cash box. Do you know anything about it?" He said he knew nothing about the missing money as he had not reconciled the funds in the box recently.

Then Mr. Curl surprised Gerry by showing him the button and asking him if it was his. Gerry examined the button and said he wasn't sure. He said, however, he was missing one just like it, and asked why? Mr. Curl told him it had been found in the cash box. He realized then that he was a suspect.

Mr. Curl was pensive. He liked Gerry - he was hard working, intelligent and had responded well to the opportunities afforded him. He was bothered by the incident but knew he must resolve it. He told Gerry he had further investigating to do, and during that period, he would be relieved of all managerial training duties. The cash box was off limits.

Gerry was crushed. He hadn't taken the money. The button had been planted in the box and he was the victim.

Preoccupied with his problem - Gerry felt he would lose his job - - all the evidence was against him. He had been set-up, but proving it was another matter.

Mr. Curl hoped his investigation would prove Gerry's innocence. However, he discovered nothing to help his situation. He related this information to Gerry and told him if no new evidence surfaced, he would be terminated.

For the past six months an interesting relationship had developed between Terrill and Mr. Curl's secretary, Veronica Walters. In consideration for certain favors, Veronica wanted Terrill's undivided devotion. Terrill, on the other hand, didn't want to ruin a good thing, so he agreed to Veronica's request. Terrill being Terrill, he had no intention of limiting his romantic excursions. As a matter of fact, he had his eye on the new bookkeeper, Izzie Fulton.

Izzie had encouraged Terrill's flirting remarks with her best smiles. She was attractively endowed and showed her cleavage with a low cut blouse. Terrill was eager to get his hands on Izzie, but he knew he must be discreet.

Mr. Curl had been looking for Terrill without success. He summoned Veronica and asked that she fetch him. The most logical place she thought would be the ice house. She reached the ice house, opened the large door and entered. She was taken back by what she saw - Terrill had Izzie on a block of ice in a compromising position. He was unperturbed saying, "Well, what is it you want snooping around down here?" Trying to recover, she said softly, "Mr. Curl wishes to see you." She turned and fled.

In recent weeks Veronica had heard Mr. Curl refer to the significance of Gerry's button. By chance, she saw Terrill place it in the cash box while simply watching and admiring him as she often did. Now, with the turn of events, she decided to have a little chat with Mr. Curl. She told him she saw Terrill place the button in the cash box. Mr. Curl knew if the information was true, Gerry was off the hook; it also meant Terrill would be demoted and maybe discharged.

Mr. Curl was caught up in the new development. While Veronica's story may have been fabricated by a jealous impulse, he found her to be honest in all her duties about the office. His best guess was her story was true. Following that, proving it could be difficult, particularly with a denial by Terrill. If push came to shove, it would be Terrill's word against Gerry's and Veronica's.

Mr. Curl decided to have all three in his office to determine who was guilty. He started the confrontation saying Gerry denied taking the money and that Veronica had seen Terrill place Gerry's button in the cash box. He then asked Terrill if he wanted to reconsider his story. Terrill said he was frustrated and fearful Gerry might vie for his position one day. It looked to him that Gerry was becoming the fair-haired boy. He had lost his head in a moment of despair and had done a very foolish thing. He then apologized to Gerry.

With his confession admitted, Mr. Curl told him he still had a job, but it would be presumptuous to think nothing had changed. His new position responsibilities would be defined shortly.

The impact of his demotion, along with the pressure of on-going scrutiny, tended to preoccupy Terrill, and he became careless in his diversion of funds scheme. In selling ice to a user, he always recorded the sale to one of the dealers who had been in just prior to the user. He charged $1.50 but recorded it as 75¢. In his carelessness, he sold to several users charging $1.50 but forgot to record them against the dealers. He still took the 75¢ for himself.

It wasn't long before Gerry discovered the shortage while reconciling the ice accounts . Further investigations disclosed Terrill's deceit.

Within two weeks, Terrill was gone and Gerry was being groomed as Mr. Curl's new assistant.

Chapter VII

1912

Gerry now twenty, was excelling as Mr. Curl's assistant, making Mr. Curl's decision prophetically correct: favoring him with new responsibilities. Phil was now working in the family store. She had graduated from high school in the top ten percentile. Her personality was an asset to the family business - giving customers the extra attention they appreciated. Actually, she liked working with the public, and it showed.

Mr. Ginetti was very happy working with Phil every day. He was proud of her integrity and her efforts to develop the business. He thought her interest in Gerry had cooled. It was time she found someone to his liking.

Antonio Damoni - now here was an up and coming young man from a good family from Julianova Beach on the Adriatic. Tony was apprenticing as a pharmacist with a bright future. Mr. and Mrs. Ginetti invited Tony to dinner, trying to arrange something between him and Phil. Phil was against the idea but decided to humor them rather than stir the embers of their old disagreement. Phil was polite and attentive, but careful not to overdo it. It was her intention not to encourage Damoni.

When she related the incident to Gerry, she dressed it up a bit, hoping to arouse a jealous reaction. It worked and Gerry became concerned, fearing Phil might become interested - it would accommodate her mother and father. They would then be one happy family.

After several days of deliberation, he decided to ask Phil to marry him. When he asked her, she said it was what she wanted.

She knew her family would never agree. Gerry said eloping would be the only alternative. They would then face the ire of the Ginettis when they returned. Gerry's mother would be disappointed not to see her only son get married. She liked Phil's considerate nature and was sure they would be happy.

They planned their elopement - the train to Elkton, Maryland, where rapid marriages were what made the town famous. Phil told her parents she and Angelo were going to Philadelphia to check a new source for meats. Angelo had agreed to this ploy; actually, he was fond of Gerry. He would really have no part in it if their parents didn't discuss it with him. They didn't.

She and Gerry left by train for Elkton. They would be married and spend a one-night honeymoon before returning the next day. She had left a note with Angelo to give her parents that evening, explaining the elopement. Mr. Ginetti said nothing.

The train ride back to Chester found Phil filled with trepidation. She knew they were going to live with Mrs. Fox, but she had to get her clothes and face her parents. Gerry tried to console her by reminiscing about their first night together. Their modesty, their fumbling first time, the wonderful expressions of love experienced through the night. These efforts helped temporarily, but her thoughts always returned to her meeting with her parents.

As they disembarked, Phil said, "I think I should go home first to see my parents and get my clothes." They walked to her home. She asked Gerry if he minded waiting until she went inside to test the water. He agreed.

Phil opened the door and went in calling, "I'm home." Her parents were in the kitchen, they heard her, but they didn't move. Phil looked in the living room and then worked her way out to the kitchen. When she saw them, she walked toward her mother, as they always embraced and kissed as a greeting. She was stopped in her tracks when her father said,"You are no longer welcome in our house." He followed with, "You are disowned." Phil looked at her mother who gave her a mournful glance then lowered her eyes. Phil burst into tears talking between sobs, "I need your support now. I love you both; I want you to love Gerry." Her father didn't look at her, but he said, "Get your clothes and leave."

Phil got her clothes and left the house. Gerry said, "You've been crying. What happened?" Phil caught her breath as she said, "They disowned me." The situation was deplorable.

Gerry suggested he talk to her parents, but Phil knew it was hopeless and it would only compound the problem.

They walked to Gerry's home with Phil's suitcase filled with her belongings. When they arrived and went in, the greeting from Mrs. Fox was the direct opposite from the one from the Ginetti's. And while Mrs. Fox was sick, she got herself up and gave them both a warm hug, telling them how pleased she was that they were home safe and sound.

Gerry was anxious to get back to work and earn money. On the other hand, Phil figured she was without a job. She mentioned to Gerry that if she heard nothing from her family, she was going to the market to work tomorrow. Hearing nothing, she went to work.

It was a trying situation at best. Her father wouldn't speak to her, but she performed her duties in the same fashion she always had. When payday came, she received her pay envelope along with the other employees. She regretted the non-communicative environment with her father, in that she was not able to talk to him, and share her thoughts and plans for the future.

Gerry's first day back to work found him enjoying his position - being married with a good job and hopefully an opportunity to assume further responsibility in the ice and coal business.

Several weeks after their marriage, Gerry stopped to see Mr. Curl before going to his desk as he came in from the ice plant. Mr. Curl complained to him of an upset stomach and mild chest pains. Gerry wasted no time calling the company doctor, Dr. Runsey. After examining Mr. Curl, Dr. Runsey said, "Herb, you have some kind of cardiac congestion, you'll have to go to the hospital where I can observe your condition further. At this point, you seem to be in no immediate danger."

A month passed. Mr. Curl was at home recuperating and making a satisfactory recovery. Gerry had assumed the responsibility of running the company with daily counselling from Mr. Curl. Gerry visited with him every morning on his way to work. The business was doing surprisingly well under Gerry's supervision. He had increased the ice and coal customers, and people liked his demeanor.

Six months to the day from the day he was stricken, Mr. Curl was returning to work when he suddenly clutched his chest as he fell at the office entrance door. He was dead before he hit the ground.

Although they were aware of his illness, all of Chester was shocked. He was well liked and looked up to as a community leader. His funeral services were attended by throngs. Mrs. Curl extended an open invitation for refreshments to everyone at her home on East Broad Street.

She spotted Gerry and Phil talking to some of the mourners. She worked her way over to them. Waiting until the conversation lagged, she asked Gerry if he could excuse himself for a few minutes and meet with her briefly.

When they were seated in Mr. Curl's small office, Mrs. Curl assured Gerry that she wanted him to continue to manage the company. She felt it was incumbent on her to learn more about the company operations, and she would rely on Gerry to help her. Gerry said he appreciated the vote of confidence and would do everything to ensure the growth and prosperity of the company.

Chapter VIII

1913

Phil remained involved at the family market, not talking to her father but still working. She saw Angelo occasionally. He indicated that their mother was depressed as a result of the family split.

Having lived such a sheltered life, she was unaware what her upset stomach in the morning meant. However, when her other feminine functions were affected, she consulted her family doctor to learn she was pregnant.

Although Gerry and she were filled with mirth, Phil was sorry she couldn't share the news with her mother. When Angelo learned of the coming event, he told their mother who asked about Phil's condition, her concern was obvious.

As the months passed, Phil continued to work and she started to show. Her father noticed her changing figure, but he remained distant. She yearned to talk to her father but knew he would stubbornly reject her.

Phil was overjoyed with her pregnancy, but the family split disturbed her. She decided to call her mother, and Angelo picked up. She asked for her mother and Angelo asked her to hold on. After a short time he returned, saying her mother would not come to the phone. He told her she was intimidated by their father, but added that she had been asking about her. They bid each other goodbye.

Thanksgiving and Christmas passed: the two most celebrated family days in the year. Even though Gerry and Mrs. Fox were considerate and loving in every way, she sorely missed her family.

February came and so did Gerry, Junior. Mother and baby both came through the delivery in fine fashion. They nicknamed Junior Kit after the offspring of the fox.

Kit got most of the attention in their little home; Gerry and his mother were in ecstasy with the new addition. They all planned and laid out his future.

In the course of their frequent discussions, Mrs. Curl asked to see Kit. Gerry was pleased with the request and arranged for Phil and Kit to join him for the next visit. Mrs. Curl served tea and layer cake while they made a fuss over the baby.

Getting to know Gerry better through their close business association, she admired not only his loyalty, but his intellect and integrity. Gerry became fond of her as well. He asked Phil if she would agree to Mrs. Curl being Kit's godmother which she did. They had already agreed that Angelo would be the godfather. They found a church to perform the baptismal service.

Several days after the baptism, there was a knock on their front door. Phil opened the door and almost collapsed - - standing there was her mother. Her mother reached out and embraced her saying, "Young lady, I could stay away no longer. I had to see you and the baby." Phil asked her what she told Dad. Mrs. Ginetti responded, "I told him I was coming to see you and the baby and if he was any kind of a father, he would join me. Believe it or not, I thought he considered it, however, he is too stubborn to give in." Phil got the baby for her mother to hold, after introducing her to Mrs. Fox. As she held Kit, he smiled at her which made his grandmother realize what she had been missing.

Mrs. Fox brewed some tea and put some cookies on the kitchen table. They all enjoyed the repast, catching up on the time they had been separated. Her mother told her how her father missed her at the market even though he wasn't speaking to her. Her absence was felt - her approach to customer relations, her diligence in getting the job done, her business ideas. No one else had the same natural talent that she had. She hoped Phil would resume her job sometime in the future because the business needed her. After several hours, Mrs. Ginetti felt it was time to leave, though she'd have liked to have stayed. She promised to return soon and hoped the day would come when they could enjoy a family dinner.

Chapter IX

Gerry had an enviable summer. The ice and coal business was expanding through his efforts: he trained his people to be courteous with the customers, his prices were competitive, and he guaranteed quick, reliable service which the customers appreciated. The happy customers were his best salespersons, spreading the word by mouth. By now he knew, no planned sales promotion performs as well as a satisfied customer.

He decided to give the ice box and heater business a try as they mixed well with his existing business. The sales were very brisk and increased the net income by fifty percent. At this point in time, it appeared the growth could be unlimited.

Mrs. Curl knew what she wanted to do. Gerry was truly running the business. He was an exceptional manager. He not only reviewed existing conditions, he studied business trends. He devised a business plan for short and long term goals. He got the most out of his employees through fairness in wages and concern for their welfare. Working conditions were as good or better than his competitors. He extended credit to worthy customers. He established a business line of credit with the Chester-Cambridge Bank, digressing from the old practice of a cash basis of operation. She realized any competitor would love to have him, but so far he was a well-kept secret. He also had the ability to open his own business with proper financial backing. With these things in mind, she proposed to Gerry that they determine the value of the business and he purchase a one-half interest. He would pay for this interest by his earned bonuses over a five year period. After this was accomplished, they would take out life insurance on each other to facilitate total ownership for the survivor. Gerry was delighted with the proposal and accepted it as presented.

As the months passed, Phil's relationship with her father did not improve. Gerry thought of intervening on her behalf. He could explain how much his daughter missed him and that his grandson would grow up without knowing his grandfather. He decided to stop at the market on the way home.

When Gerry approached the market, he saw someone dashing out the door. He entered the door and saw a man with a gun at the counter demanding Mr. Ginetti to open the cash register. He refused, telling the gunman to get out of his store. Gerry stood where he was, not wanting to excite the robber into a shooting spree. Without any further hesitation, the gunman fired at Mr. Ginetti hitting him in the shoulder. He was moving to go over the counter when Gerry made a flying tackle, knocking him to the floor. Gerry was all over him, forcing the gun out of his hand and grabbing the hair on the top of his head, pulling back and slamming his face down onto the floor. He repeated this five times, knocking the robber senseless. By then, the person who ran out of the market had found a policeman who entered the market with gun drawn. Gerry left the robber and went over to check Mr. Ginetti. He was bleeding badly from the wound and was semi-conscious. As the policeman put the cuffs on the robber, Gerry ran out to get Dr. Tiboletti who lived two doors away. After emergency treatment, Mr. Ginetti was taken to the Chester Hospital where the bullet was removed, and he was assigned a room.

He was kept in the hospital for three days to monitor the low grade fever which accompanied an infection caused by the wound. During that time, his wife told him of Gerry's quick reaction in the market, that he most likely saved his life as it appeared the robber was about to shoot him again.

Mr. Ginetti, through his wife, said he wished to see both Phil and Gerry. When they entered his room, Mr. Ginetti greeted them saying, "Hello, Phil, I'ma glad you came."

His daughter went to the bed and gave him a prolonged hug saying, "I've missed you terribly Daddy. Are you feeling better?" He answered that he was. He then said, "Hello, Mr. Fox. Thanka you for sava my life. I could have been a goner."

Gerry said, "I didn't know where you were shot till I got over beside you. I was relieved to see it had not hit a vital organ. Even so, the blood was pumping out. Thank God for Dr. Tiboletti."

Mr. Ginetti asked, "How'sa my grandson?"

Phil assured him he was in fine health.

Phil knew now that her father would soon be playing with Kit.

Chapter X

1924

Kit had turned ten and his family had just purchased and moved onto a forty-two acre farm in the Lima area of Middletown, some eight miles north of Chester. Gerry Sr.'s love for horses had provoked the move. The farm had a stable of five thoroughbreds and a quarter horse for Kit.

Many events had taken place in the past decade. Gerry's mother, Mrs. Fox, had passed on. Mrs. Curl had gone to her final reward, and Gerry was now the sole owner of the ice and coal business. As a result, his worth had grown considerably.

Chester was growing industrially with factories popping up along the Delaware River. The downtown area had grown into the business hub of southern Delaware County. The area's transportation needs were serviced by rail and trolleys locally.

World War I was fought and won by the United States and her allies and the League of Nations was formed to prevent a repeat of such a worthless exercise in the future.

The Model "T" was getting to be a familiar sight, having been produced by Henry Ford, the inventor of the automobile assembly line. People were actually getting from one place to another by automobile as well as by trolleys and trains.

Fox Lair, as the farm was named, had a spacious two-and-a-half story farmhouse. The clapboard was painted white, the shutters forest green and Phil had furnished it with an Early American theme. The house welcomed everyone with its friendly atmosphere.

Gerry and Kit rose early, taking their horses for a short morning ride. They both loved these jaunts, racing, chatting with father and son camaraderie. Kit was a born equestrian. He seemed to take naturally to everything about horses.

They were on the last turn of their morning run when the quarter horse shied. Kit, surprised by the sudden move, fell off and hit his head on a honeycomb rock. He lay on the ground not moving. Gerry dismounted and ran over to him. Kit had some blood on his head. He was unconscious. Gerry looked him over carefully, then went to his canteen, wet his bandanna and he put it on Kit's forehead. After a few minutes, his eyes fluttered as he came to.

Kit moved very slowly into a sitting position, asking his dad what had happened. As his dad explained, Kit complained that he felt dizzy. His dad's advice was to stay put for a while. After a few minutes passed, he was ready to climb back up in the saddle.

By the time they finished their ride home, the bleeding had stopped, and Kit went to the kitchen to wash up and clean his injury. Gerry thought to himself how tough his kid was. Most ten-year-olds would cry all the way home, not thinking of mounting the quarter horse again.

All Saturdays were always a festive time, especially in the summer. Gerry went to the business until 1:00 P.M. When he came home and changed, it was time for a ride. Usually, some of the neighbors were visiting, so they joined in the activities. There was a short, fenced riding ring with jumps arranged to demonstrate a horse and rider's skill. Many times when riding and jumping in the jumping ring, a rider would get thrown, sometimes breaking ribs and other bones.

After the riding exhibit, everyone would settle down for a cookout with a roasted pig or piece of beef, baked potatoes (cooked in the coals), and fresh vegetable salad. Phil would bake a cherry or apple pie and a vanilla layer cake with rich chocolate icing. The cookout would continue until dark and then all would move inside, and Phil would play the piano while everyone sang, laughed and jigged.

One Saturday afternoon, Bungy found his way to Fox Lair. His appearance was unexpected. As it turned out, his reason for coming had a purpose. Tata had been arrested and charged with breaking and entering and the theft of a diamond bracelet and a ruby dress pin surrounded by diamonds.

"Did he do it?" Gerry asked.

"He says he didn't, but they found the jewelry in his house. The owner claims she first missed it last night," replied Bungy. He continued, "The police got an anonymous note tipping them off regarding the gems which had been stolen and where they were stashed."

The next day Gerry questioned Tata, who vehemently denied taking the jewelry. He said, "I had no knowledge of how the jewelry got in my home." Either Tata was lying or the jewelry had been planted there with the possibility of the thief retrieving it at a later date.

The police were confident that Tata was guilty. Gerry was inclined to believe Tata. He found him to be truthful over the years. However, he may have been covering for someone else.

Tata had no clue what to do; he didn't know what was required to prepare his defense. He was confused by the entire matter.

Tata's younger sister, Elizabeth, nicknamed Queenie, was eighteen and at a vulnerable time of her life. Tata did his best to steer her straight, but Queenie resented his efforts; she thought he really knew nothing about today's way of life. Wanting to do her thing with her new boyfriend, she needed no interference from her bossy brother. The more space she wanted and took, the more difficult he became. She wanted to stay out late with her boyfriend, Squeak, and do things, he said, all the other girls did.

Queenie's feelings for Tata were developing into hatred. She decided to enlist Squeak's help in getting rid of her brother.

She had a friend who did domestic work for one of the more wealthy Chester families. In the course of conversation, she had mentioned the jewelry collection her mistress had amassed. And as time passed, she said she wouldn't be working the following week; her people would be away.

Queenie got hold of Squeak and told him her plan. Squeak, a thief by nature, was to sneak into the home while the folks were on vacation and steal what jewels he could find. In return for his efforts, he could take his pleasure with her whenever he pleased as Tata would no longer be around. She would plant the jewelry so that he would get the blame.

The caper went off quite well since Squeak had no trouble picking the lock. He let himself into the house and searched the master bedroom for a jewelry box. Spotting it on the dressing table, he went over, opened it and helped himself to the diamond bracelet and the ruby dress pin.

Queenie had to talk Squeak out of fencing the jewels. She eventually succeeded and planted them in Tata's room.

When the owner discovered the missing jewels, she told her husband and called the Chester Police Department, reporting the burglary.

The Chester Times' crime reporter had a small account of the incident in his column. Queenie had been waiting for the squib; when she saw it, she went into action. She and Squeak prepared an anonymous note indicating Tata was the burglar. The note was written in unmatching letters cut out of the Saturday Evening Post and sent to the City police captain.

The police quickly called at Tata's family's house. Tata's mother answered the door, and replied that Tata was not home. Armed with a search warrant, they asked where his room was. They spent more than an hour searching, finally locating the jewels hidden in an old pair of shoes in the rear of Tata's clothes closet.

When Tata came home, the police were waiting. They told Tata he was under arrest for breaking and entering and stealing the jewels which they showed him. They cuffed him and took him to the police station for questioning.

At the station they led him into the interrogation room. Tata reiterated that he had never seen the jewels, that he didn't know who owned them, or where they came from. The police persisted, wanting to know when he broke in, how he sprung the lock, and how he knew the owners would be away. Tata insisted he knew nothing. He ended up being indicted with his bail at $1,000.

Queenie's plan was falling into place. The evidence against her brother was substantial and should hold up for a conviction. She felt she was now able to run her own life with no interference from Tata.

After Gerry put up Tata's bail, they reviewed how he could have gotten implicated. Gerry finally said what they both had been thinking, "Queenie must have been involved."

Tata's love for his sister inhibited his desire to implicate her, but who else knew where to hide the jewels? What was her reasoning? Did she really dislike him so thoroughly to set him up? How could she have gotten the jewels?

Queenie was tiring of Squeak. She thought him a braggadocios bore. There was no excitement about him. He never took her anywhere. All he wanted to do was try to get her to drop her pants. She decided to look for greener pasture. Each time Squeak tried to see her, she put him off. He became very annoyed.

Chapter XI

Mark Terrill was now married, rather loosely. He expected his wife to overlook his indiscretions while he overlooked his marriage vows.

Walking up Market Street, he noticed the flirtatious Queenie looking directly at him. He gave her a wink, and she smiled provocatively. Approaching her, he struck up a conversation; as one thing led to another, he asked her to join him for a birch beer over at Birney's.

Seated in a booth, she asked Mark about himself. Being an egotist and short on the truth, he led her to believe he was a man of means. He explained that he was married but had few family obligations. He said, "Come to think of it, I may just leave the old shrew." Queenie's interest was peaked.

Actually, old Terrill could barely make ends meet, but Queenie, being young and gullible, took his line - hook, line and sinker. She thought Terrill a handsome man-about-town and encouraged his attention. As they finished their drinks, Terrill asked if she knew the big willow tree down by Chester Creek in Deshong Park; she did and they arranged a meeting on Tuesday after dinner.

Tuesday evening found Queenie waiting by the big willow. She had been waiting for a half hour and now feared he may not show. Ten minutes later she saw him walking toward her. When he reached the tree, they exchanged warm greetings and walked until they found a park bench by the creek.

The weather was warm, and the sun was setting allowing cool air to float up to them from the water. They were never at a loss for words which put them at ease. While Queenie was talking, Terrill casually put his arm on the back of the bench and she moved closer to him. He looked at her face which was tilted up toward his. He suddenly brushed her lips with his. Queenie seized the chance and threw her arms around his neck and gave him a kiss which quickly turned into one of French passion. She willingly gave him preliminary liberties. As each became more aroused, he suggested she remove her panties. She quickly answered; "You're in luck, I've left them home." Mark, the experienced lover, quickly moved her into a compromising position. Still on the bench, she found herself stretched out under him half on and half off the bench doing a bit of a balancing act while trying to perform. In the heat of the act, Queenie lost her balance, landing them both on the ground, his weight knocking the wind out of her, quickly ending their love making effort. Queenie got up, brushed herself off and remarked, "Mark, won't you find a spot where we might have a softer landing?"

Squeak was in a miserable mood. He had been had by that conniving Queenie. He robbed the jewels, risked being caught and now she dumped him before he got his due. What a fool! And what if she decided to squeal, putting the blame on him. He wouldn't take it lying down.

He planned his revenge. She deserved a good working over. He told her he had heard a new development about her brother; it was imperative he see her to discuss it. They met at the B&O train station in the evening. Squeak suggested they go around to the back of the station so as not to be conspicuous. As soon as they stepped into the darkness, he beat her soundly and severely leaving her unconscious on the ground.

When Queenie came to, her nose was bleeding, her eyes were swollen into slits, and her ribs felt broken. She had difficulty swallowing. She finally got up thinking - I'm ending up on the ground one way or the other. She wandered home where Tata saw her condition.

Tata asked who beat her? Queenie was in a dilemma: if she pointed a finger, Squeak might say she stole the jewels; if she didn't talk, Tata would surmise it was Squeak and take the matter into his own hands. She kept quiet.

Tata decided to hunt Squeak down. He inquired at the local hangouts - no luck. Where was the gutless guttersnipe? He ran into Bungy outside the Chester National Bank and inquired if he knew anything of Squeak's whereabouts. Bungy hadn't seen Squeak but heard he was insinuating that Queenie pulled the jewel heist. Bungy was to keep him informed of any news on Squeak.

Tata knew he'd get him, but when?

Finally, Bungy got a lead; Squeak was to be at the new 9th Street diner to meet with some small-time Philadelphia hustlers Friday, around supper time.

Tata got himself down to the diner and spotted Squeak at his meeting. He decided to wait 'til he came out. There was an overgrown area between the diner and Chester Creek where he decided to hide.

Around 7:30, he saw Squeak get up and go over to the cashier to pay his bill. Tata left his hiding spot and came to the side of the diner. As Squeak came out and started to walk up 9th Street, Tata grabbed him by the front of his jacket and pulled him stumbling back behind the diner. Squeak said, "What the hell ..." when Tata's ham size fist interrupted him, crushing into his face with a sickening thud, spreading his nose. "That's for beating on my sister." As Squeak started to slip down the wall of the diner, Tata hammered a right into his solar plexus. Squeak doubled over grabbing his stomach thinking he would die. He couldn't breathe. Tata wasn't finished: he straightened him up against the diner, opened his hands and smashed both Squeak's ears a terrible blow with the palms of his hands, making a loud clapping sound. Then with startling quickness shot pulverizing blows, a right to the left rib cage and a left to the right. Squeak crumbled. Tata left him on the ground with his face a bloody pulp, his body aching.

Chapter XII

As Tata's hearing approached, he and Gerry felt sure Queenie was involved along with Squeak. Only Queenie would have hidden the jewels in Tata's shoes; she was also seeing Squeak then. Tata didn't want to implicate his sister knowing prison would simply encourage her bad tendencies.

Gerry told Tata it would do Queenie no good for him to take the rap. She would just fall more quickly into her wayward habits, and who knew what Squeak would do to her in his absence. Also, if Squeak took part in the theft, he had a debt to pay to society. Gerry was going to confront Queenie.

At the meeting, Queenie denied everything. However, when Gerry told her Squeak was saying she stole the jewels and hid them in her brother's shoes, she said, "That rotten rat squealer stole the jewels! All I did was hide the damn things."

Queenie's problems were compounding. Born of Cockney parents, Mark Terrill's wife was a tough little bundle. Pretty as a picture, honest and a one-maner. They named her Shiela, for her maternal grandmother.

Growing tired of Mark's indiscretions, the lipstick on his shirt, the foreign perfume on his coat, Sheila decided to perform her own investigation.

Queenie, with her world collapsing, wanted to see her handsome Romeo, Mark. She arranged a rendezvous at the canoe shed at Ships Creek.

Queenie tried to cover her bruises with makeup. She only did a mediocre job. When she arrived at the shed, Mark was already waiting. They both liked the canoe shed: the rental canoes were stored there, equipped with mattresses to accommodate the lovers renting them for an evening ride up or down the creek. The owners of the canoe concession were closing it as it was no longer turning a profit. Consequently, the canoes were just sitting in the shed waiting their final disposition. What a great spot for a love nest, Queenie thought, no one else knew of it.

Mark, suave, handsome, crafty, and sneaky, ushered Queenie into the shed. Luckily, the twilight hid her facial cover up. Seeing he had already picked a comfy canoe, she thought, no chance of falling off the bench this time. Setting preliminaries aside, they cuddled down in the canoe and got right to the business at hand. With Queenie on bottom, her gartered silk stockinged legs astride, their passions took over. They encouraged each other with moans and groans, humping and bumping in the old canoe. Suddenly, a bright beam was on them and Shiela snarled, "Mark, you two-timing phoney, get off that tramp and go home while I deal with her." Mark was so shocked he did just what she ordered. Shiela's next move came so quickly it shocked Queenie. As Queenie struggled to get up, Shiela jumped her, pulling strands of her hair out, and biting her shoulder, she drew blood. Queenie tried to fight back, but Shiela was all over her, scratching, punching, slapping and kicking. Queenie, in the bottom of the canoe, was at her mercy and soon Shiela got off her, yelling, "Keep away from my man, whore, or the next time it'll be worse."

Queenie's star was fading, beaten up twice in a week, and she was facing incarceration.

Squeak was not faring much better, he was in the same boat.

Chapter XIII

1926

Kit was twelve and growing. Actually, he was big for his age. His good looks were developing; he inherited his dark curly hair from his mother and his blue eyes from his dad. He had a scar on his cheek from a throw he took from his horse, giving him a rugged appearance. Kit would be entering seventh grade in the fall.

It was summertime and Gerry rented a cottage in Lewes, Delaware, for a two-week vacation. Known originally as a fishing village with a fish factory which supported it, vacationers started coming to enjoy swimming, boating and fishing because of the natural beach on the Delaware Bay.

The family packed up the Studebaker touring car to start their trip. The suitcases were placed on the running board and held there by a metal adjustable gate. Packing sandwiches and lemonade for lunch, they looked for a spot where they could stop to picnic along the way.

They arrived at Lewes about an hour after lunch. The cottage was across the street from the beach. It was a seasonal cedar shingle two-story typical summer cottage. The living room had a brick fireplace, the dining room and kitchen were both good size. The second floor had three double bedrooms and a plain bath. They were pleased, feeling it would be a very comfortable two weeks. The outstanding feature was the screened front porch with its high backed rockers, perfect for rocking and watching the beach activity and the fishing boats as they returned with the catch of the day.

They arrived on Sunday, everything was fine and dandy. They went to the beach for a dip. Kit loved the water and was a good swimmer, having learned in the fresh water pond at home. After the swim, they cleaned up and played an old card game called "I Doubt It."

Monday morning, they awakened to a terrible smell. The fish factory had been closed on Sunday, but it was unmistakenly open now. If the prevailing wind was from the southwest, the surrounding homes got the full-blown sickening odor. No one had mentioned this unfortunate situation. They later learned that the rents were reasonable because of the smell. Now they understood why the beach was seldom crowded.

The Delaware Bay was enormous, and at Lewes, it resembled the ocean without the large breakers unless there was a nor'easter. On occasion, there were huge schools of jellyfish with long tentacles resembling the Portuguese man-o-war. The tentacles gave a severe sting.

Gerry and Kit rented a rowboat and Gerry rowed out a hundred yards or so; they dropped their lines and caught dinner in no time. It was a fisherman's paradise. Always delighted with their catch of the day, Phil pan fried the fish, boiled the potatoes, garnished with butter and parsley, and served with golden bantam corn on the cob. How they loved those fish dinners.

Kit made friends with Jack Horn, the youngster next door. They enjoyed many of the same things, swimming, fishing and peanut butter sandwiches. Kit taught Jack how to play "I Doubt It," and he joined the family games. When they weren't out fishing, they spent time on the beach and swimming in the bay.

A stationary raft was positioned a short swim off shore. The younger set swam to it where they sunned, chatted and frolicked, jumping and diving into the bay.

Kit and Jack spent the early part of the morning on the beach, playing ball, building sand castles and searching the beach for nature's treasures. Jack noticed the raft was deserted and said, "Come on, let's race out to the raft." They plunged into the water and were on their way. Both swam the crawl but had to change to a less tiring stroke. Jack was the first to return to the crawl and ended up winning by a stroke. They climbed the ladder and collapsed on the deck with

Kit saying, "I'll beat you on the way back." They sat up and talked while they rested. It wasn't long until they used the diving board. Their efforts included a flip, jack knife and swan dive. In a rating from one to ten, they scored threes and fours. On Jack's last attempt at a swan dive he came up with a jellyfish on his head and tentacles stuck to his face. The stinging was excruciating, and Jack was screaming. He didn't know what it was and he swatted at his face and head with both hands. With his hands busy, he was unable to tread water and slipped under the surface. Kit dove off the raft directly toward the spot where Jack had gone under. He grabbed but felt nothing, then he brushed Jack's shoulder. His lungs felt as though they would burst. He grabbed Jack's armpit and pulled him with him as he surfaced. Jack panicked and wrapped his arms around Kit's neck. The jellyfish was off, but Jack's face was welted from the tentacles. Kit tried to pry loose as they went under again, but being face to face made it difficult to break away. Again out of breath, he was near panic. He got his hands under Jack's arms and pushed up, ducking his head out of the grip. He surfaced while holding onto one of Jack's arms. Surprisingly, he was beside the raft and he grabbed it with his free hand. Jack suddenly relaxed when he saw the raft; he quit thrashing and let Kit pull him toward safety. His strength gone, Kit had been ready to give up. Jack would have drowned.

With no life saving training, Kit had acted on instinct. He showed incredible courage saving Jack.

When they eventually headed toward the beach, instead of diving, they eased themselves into the water and swam cautiously, avoiding a few jellyfish along the way. By the time they reached the beach, they were both exhausted from their earlier ordeal. Jack said, "I never panicked like that in my life but I never had a jellyfish perched on my head. The welts are killing me. I'm going home to see what my mother can do to ease the stinging." When his mother saw him, she rushed him to the local doctor where Jack was treated and sent home.

The next day Gerry took Kit and Jack fishing. Jack still showed evidence of the welts, but the sting had subsided. Gerry got them started rowing away from the beach. Then Kit gave it a try. This vacation gave him his first opportunity to row. He pulled harder with his right arm and, not seeing where they were going, kept the boat moving to the left of center. Eventually, he realized he was no longer facing the land when all he saw was water. He kept pulling with his right arm until he had completed a 360° turn about. Now he tried to balance the pull with each arm and pulled the boat straight out into the bay. When it was Jack's turn he took over with no trouble at all. He learned from Kit's turn.

They dropped their lines when Gerry thought they reached a hole the old timers talked about. While Gerry and Jack each caught a couple of fluke, Kit wasn't having much luck although something did steal his bait a few times. Then suddenly, he had a heavy pull; he jerked his line securing the hook in his catch. Whatever was on his line kept swimming back and forth, tugging strenuously. The fish pulled so hard he almost lost the line. Gerry told him to let some out. He did and the fish took it. When the line slackened, he snapped the reel, stopping the line, and it went taut. Kit said, "I hope the fish is wearing out because I am."

The fish struggled - thrashing back and forth in a herky jerky motion. Kit was losing his grip. Gerry saw what was happening and grabbed the rod; he had trouble getting a grip on it while the fish fought to survive. He reeled in a bit more, he handed the rod back to Kit. Kit did what he'd seen his father do - play with the fish then reel in. The fish seemed to be tiring, Kit was able to reel in more line. Except for a tug now and then, he continued to reel in. Just when it appeared it was all over, the fish took off again. Kit finally got control and reeled the fighter in without much effort. As he pulled him up to the surface, the flat head appeared with knobs on either end. As everyone got into the act, Gerry said, "My God, it's a hammerhead shark." They brought the hammer into the boat with its hammerhead going back and forth rapidly. Gerry took the big fish off the hook and threw him back in the bay saying, "Son, that was some catch. It's not often you catch a hammer."

"Dad, it's something I won't forget, I almost lost the rod and reel to that old fighter." Enough fishing for one day, they headed back to the beach.

The rest of the vacation passed quickly. Lewes offered an interesting two weeks, and the Fox family took every moment of excitement and relaxation they could. Kit and Jack made the usual promises to keep in touch. Jack's family lived in Wilmington, fifteen miles from Lima. Interestingly enough, they did keep in touch.

Chapter XIV

1930-31

Kit's senior year was eventful: he captained the track team, played first team end on the football team, went to the senior prom and graduated from Media High School with good grades.

He was accepted at Waterville Military Academy. He never considered any other. The military, the cavalry, polo and Gerry influenced his decision. Gerry was as happy as Kit: had he had the opportunity, he'd have been a cadet in a heart beat.

In the past year, Kit acquired a polo mallet and ball and began working on basic fundamentals: learning to strike the ball while riding his horse, practicing the quick turns and the stop and go maneuvers.

Gerry realized Kit's potential as a polo player. To help develop this, Gerry purchased a polo pony. These unusual horses not only were specially trained but had instinctive abilities to stop and start quickly, turn on a dime and respond to the rider's command with dispatch. When Kit mounted his pony, they were almost molded together. The pony's name was perfect - "Win".

The summer before Kit entered WMA, he worked at the family business and spent most of his free time working with Win.

At sundown, he and Win were just completing their workout. Mary Lou was leaning on the post and rail separating their properties. "Kit, I want to help you groom Win." Mary Lou Folkner was two years younger than Kit, long-limbed, blue-eyed, brunette, with room to fill out. Tomboyish, she liked hanging around Kit, sharing his activities on the farm. She was an excellent equestrian, and they rode the area together. Mary Lou's interest was more than the rough and tumble times; she had a teen-age crush on Kit, but he was oblivious to her feelings.

They brushed Win down; how handsome he was, coat shining, white boots and a star on his forehead. He loved Kit and was warming up to Mary Lou, but only tolerated other people. When Kit was standing near but paying him no heed, Win would nudge him until he drew his attention. The better they got to know each other and work together, the more each understood the other.

The heat of August, the dry weather and the dog days starting to shorten meant the summer was passing. College would be commencing, and Kit was excited. Mary Lou, on the other hand, was unhappy knowing he was going to live at college and she would see less of him.

What Mary Lou enjoyed most were the tennis matches they played which she usually won. Her dad was a respectable player and they frequently played on their own court. He had started Mary Lou playing as a young girl. She soon became adept with a great serve, a good forehand, and a backhand that needed some work. With her development into a rangy teenager, her stature complimented her game. Each year she improved and while Kit played well, his interest never approached Mary Lou's.

On a Saturday morning in August, they played a lively match, and each won a set. In the third set Mary Lou was leading five to three as she had broken service once. Kit was serving and down 30-40. His first serve was just in but over near the doubles line. Mary Lou ran, stretched and returned the shot deep. Kit's return was a hard forehand; Mary Lou returned a drop shot just over the net which literally died. Kit ran but couldn't get to it. Mary Lou was thrilled; she ran and jumped the net, shaking Kit's hand with a laugh. Kit put a friendly arm around her saying, "You are one fine tennis player. Do you ever lose?"

Mary Lou answered, "Of course I lose, I just don't want to lose to you." She loved the hug and wished it could be more, that she were older and a lot more appealing. Kit broke it off saying, "Win and I are going to work out."

"I'd love to learn to play polo, why not let me play the opposition?"

"You don't have a polo pony. Our other horses can't maneuver adroitly enough."

"If you have a second mallet, I'd love to try it on your old quarter horse. He's smart and quick, I think he'd manage. Let's try it."

Kit had another old mallet and agreed they give it a go. He insisted Mary Lou get the protector helmet before they actually started banging the ball.

With Mary Lou fully attired and astride, Kit stuck the ball and charged after it on Win. Mary Lou was in full chase on the quarter, but Kit easily out maneuvered them as the quarter was no match for Win. When Kit suggested Mary Lou try it alone, she did and surprised Kit being quite apt for a beginner. He wondered what she might have done on Win.

They had great times emulating chukkers. Occasionally, Kit let Mary Lou ride Win, and she performed well. She told Kit if WMA were coed, she'd go there and try out for the team. As it was, she'd settle for the matches they created and was thankful for the time they spent together.

The summer passed finally, and Kit could barely wait for classes to start. He drove to Chester to look the campus over. He found a parking spot and walked past "Old Main" to the stadium and entered through a ramp where he could view the activity field used for cadet parades, football, polo, baseball and commencement exercises. He visualized the polo players racing up and down the field, hoping he would be one of them. Knowing many of the polo players brought their own ponies, he hoped to bring Win with him.

Chapter XV

The plebes reported earlier than the upper classmen to receive uniforms and indoctrination. Rooms and roommates were also assigned. Kit's roommate was Freddie Burner, a handsome tennis player with a flare that attracted girls. As it turned out, he would be a loyal friend, a dedicated soldier and a good student. "Old Main" housed most of the activities: the first floor housed administration offices and the auditorium, the second and third floors were the dormitories, and classrooms were on the fourth floor. The floor at ground level contained the mess hall, post office and heating equipment. The college was easily identified by its proud edifice. "Old Main," an imposing structure with a white painted dome, was visible for miles.

The plebes were billeted on the third floor and the upper classmen on the second. Certain officers of the corp returned with the plebes to oversee their settling in, as it were.

Kit and Freddie were stowing their recently issued gear when an upper classmen walked into their room. Both turned and looked at the lieutenant. Freddie said, "Hi." The lieutenant looked at them scornfully and said, "On your feet and stand at attention when an officer presents himself. Chest out, chin in, eyes straight ahead, feet together. Now hold the position for two minutes." He turned and left the room; they stood at attention.

At the first free moment Kit had, he went down to the riding hall to see the polo ponies and the cavalry horses. Most of the ponies were specially trained quarter horses and had the acute reflexes required in polo competition.

An old groom came out from one of the stalls and eyed Kit, "What are you lookin' for son?"

"I'm interested in polo and I wanted to look around. I'm Kit Fox. I hope to make the polo team."

"My name's Jake, I'll show you around." As they roamed through, Jake said, "We beat Princeton, Harvard, Yale and Army in 1927. Won the national indoor intercollegiate championship. They were all good players, one was the great Newt Wyman, now a doctor, really some polo player."

Kit was fascinated with Jake's stories, the ponies and the facilities. He was eager to find out how his skills stacked up under actual competition. He learned that of the thirty ponies required, several were owned by the more affluent players. Kit wondered if he might bring Win in if and when he made the team. He could barely wait for the indoor season practice commencing in October.

When he got back to the room, Freddie was standing at attention. Lieutenant Downs had just left, instructing him regarding the two minute drill.

When classes started, the daily routine was reveille at 5:30 A.M., breakfast at 6:00, muster and drill from 7:00 until 8:00, classes from 8:30 to 11:15, lunch at noon, classes from 1:15 to 3:30. From 4:00 to 6:00, athletic practice, rifle range, cavalry and other military duties were scheduled. Dinner was at 6:30, study was from 7:30 to 10:00 and taps at 10:45 P.M. The cadets slept well.

Saturday afternoons were spent attending intercollegiate games or matches. At football games the corps marched on the field then filed into the stands and remained as a unit until the game was over. Saturday evenings were date nights: proms, balls and movies. If a cadet was dating a girl from Chester, he had to choose from the girls registered socially with the college. On Sunday the cadets were required to march to churches located in the City.

The college enrollment was about one hundred and fifty. The residents of Chester loved to see these fine young cadets march through the City streets in perfect cadence; the future custodians of the nation's military welfare.

Chapter XVI

Kit was taken with everything about the college: the military training, the cavalry, the camaraderie of the corps, polo, the professor's personal student interest in the small classrooms and esprit de corps.

One of the military games enjoyed most by the corps was the sham battle in which actual battle conditions were simulated. While all the ammunition were blanks, the bellowing of cannons, the cracking of rifles, the charging of cavalry, the attacks and retreats were all very realistic. Invariably, these sham battles were performed on the activity field in front of spectators in the grand stands. They looked forward to these real battle dramas as much as the corps did.

Kit's eventual interest in ordnance developed from the sham battle games. Little did he know that this interest would eventually lead to a critical occurrence in his life.

When polo practice commenced, Kit was among the rest of the players. All were veterans, except the four newcomers trying to make the team. Only two of the four would be carried: one of the newcomers was on scholarship and one of the other three would make it. Harvey Beels was on the scholarship; Joe McKee, Al Tyler and Kit were the other three. Joe McKee loved the game but lacked talent. Al Tyler and Kit had unproven ability; they would start out as equals.

At practice, the four worked on fundamentals. Harvey was good; he had some experience and it showed. Al went out of his way to make Kit look bad, elaborating on his errors, and cottoning up to the coach.

Eventually, they were worked into practice chukkers. Joe was the first to be cut. Al and Kit were on opposing practice teams, both riding down the wooden ball. Al had a shot. As he got ready to swing, Kit rode up and hooked his mallet, preventing the shot. Al fell from his pony; lying on the ground, he feigned his breath was knocked out of him. Kit rode over and dismounted to offer assistance. Al acted as if he could not breathe. Finally, he rolled over choking, "Why did you hook my leg, unbalancing me? You made me fall. That was a dirty play."

Kit said, "I only hooked your mallet, you faked that spill you took."

Al replied, "If you can't compete without foul play, you shouldn't be out here."

The coach yelled over, "If everyone's O.K. over there, let's get back to work."

Al rode over to the coach and said, "I'm ready if he doesn't take any more cheap shots at me." Kit never heard the remark, he had already resumed practice.

Kit and Al were competing evenly for the last spot on the team. Al continued to shine the apple with the coach. When the choice was made, Al got the spot because of his butt-kissing not because of his superior polo talent.

Kit was disappointed, but his spirit wasn't broken. He continued to have a presence at the riding hall. When one of the players was unable to attend practice, he was permitted to fill the void.

On one of these occasions, Al caught up with Kit after practice, he said, "Don't ever try a trick like the one the other day."

"I never hooked your leg. I hooked your mallet to make you miss the shot. Your spill was phonied by you to make me look bad. It seems to have worked since you made the team."

"Come on Kit, you couldn't shine my boots, I can ride circles around you; you just don't have it."

"Don't worry Tyler, my turn will come, don't be surprised when I outscore you." Leaving Al standing there, Kit went over to the mess hall.

When Kit entered the mess hall, he spotted Freddie. He went over and joined him for supper.

Freddie greeted him, "Did you get to ride today?"

"Yes, I got a little action in, two of the regulars were out with upset stomachs. I rode with Tyler. God, how I want to ride against him. He always has a few choice words for me. Tries to discourage me. But it makes me try harder."

"Don't worry, you'll get your chance. Just be patient, I know it'll come." Freddie dug his fork into his mashed potatoes.

"How's your backhand these days?" Kit asked, reaching for his milk.

"My backhand's better than my service. Coach has me playing number five position. I think I can beat all the guys ahead of me except Wright. He's a fine tennis player. I'm spending extra time on my service; it's improving. Playing number five, I think I'll win my share of matches."

"I have a friend at home, a girl named Mary Lou. She's a good tennis player; maybe when you visit us sometime, you and she can enjoy a match."

"Set it up when we have a furlough, I'll be ready anytime.

"Kit, do you believe fate takes a hand in the events of life?"

"Yes, I do."

Fate moved in strange ways, it was making its move.

Chapter XVII

One of the players that had stomach ailments turned out to have a burst appendix and required immediate surgery to prevent peritonitis. The other had a short stay in the dispensary under the expert care of the beloved nurse - Annie Collins.

This turn of events moved Kit up to the eight man squad. Tyler was livid.

Not having made the team, Kit was unable to bring his own pony. Now he was allowed to bring Win aboard.

Win and Kit were like one with Kit in the saddle. In competition, the players changed ponies frequently because of the gruelling exercise. Kit would not ride Win all the time; when he did, he made the most of it.

As the practice continued, Coach Fisher became more and more impressed with Kit. His talent was developing quickly, and Win was something else on the polo field. He instinctively knew the positioning Kit expected him to take.

By the time they played their first match, Kit worked his way up to second substitute right behind Harvey Beels. The match was at home, and against a great Army team, traveling down from West Point. The entire team had the pre-match anxiety, which luckily passed the moment the action started.

Al couldn't resist taking a shot at Kit just before the match. He said, "You got lucky lately, it won't last. After Mahoney gets well, you'll be looking in from the outside."

Kit looked at him challenging, "My plans are to stay on the team; now that I've made it, you can bet on it." The confrontation ended with Kit staring him down.

Gerry, Phil and Mary Lou came to see the match. Anxious to see Kit, Mary Lou talked Gerry and Phil into taking her with them. Actually, it was no problem as they liked her and her company.

When Kit saw Mary Lou, he thought she and Freddie could play a tennis match. What a natural . . they're both good. He suggested it to her, but she'd have no part of it. She came to see Kit, whether he played or not. She could tell he was oblivious to her feelings.

The match was going into the last chukker tied at one apiece when the coach decided to try Kit. He was ready with Win. They played exactly the way they had in practice. They were at the right place at the right time. Suddenly, he out-raced an opponent, thundered down the field, and he whacked the ball through the posts for a goal. WMA beat Army 2 to 1.

On the sidelines, his team mates were congratulating him as Mary Lou, his dad and mom arrived to express their pleasure at his performance. Tyler stalked off, saying nothing.

The Thanksgiving holiday came quickly. Shortly after Kit got home to enjoy all the festivities, Mary Lou walked over for a visit. When Kit looked at her, it was like he had been blind and suddenly gotten his sight back. She was beautiful and maturing into quite a young lady. She came over and gave him a hug, and for the first time, he affectionately returned the favor. Pleasantly surprised, she said, "That felt good, I miss you when you're away."

He found himself saying, "I miss you, too. Always under my feet, beating me at tennis and riding a pretty good horse.

"Next Saturday our football team plays Delaware in Atlantic City at Convention Hall. The corps parades down the boardwalk and into Convention Hall preceding the game. Mom and Dad are coming, why don't you join them? It's quite unique, playing football indoors."

"Let's see. I'll have to rearrange a date Saturday night if I can. He's not a happy camper when I change his plans."

"Who is this dude?. Or are you pulling my leg?"

Smiling, she said, "It was worth a try, wasn't it?"

Mary Lou said she'd love to come along; she hadn't been to Atlantic City for several years. The cadets were billeted at the Claridge Hotel, and Gerry and Phil also had made their accommodations there.

The night of the game, the cadets were impressive marching down the boardwalk in perfect cadence. When they got to Convention Hall, they marched into a rousing ovation.

After the game, the cadets had until midnight before reporting back to the Claridge. Gerry, Phil, Kit and Mary Lou went to the Knife and Fork for a late snack. As they were finishing up, Kit noticed a familiar face a few tables away. Sure enough, it was Jack Horn, his friend from their Lewes holiday. He got up and approached Jack's table. When Jack saw Kit, he broke into a smile and got up to meet him. They embraced and Kit said, "It's been ages since we've corresponded. What are you doing in Atlantic City?"

"The same thing you are. I came here to watch Delaware beat WMA. Which they did. Too bad we didn't have a little bet. I'm a freshman at the University of Delaware. So you decided on the military. How do you like it?"

"I like it just fine. I'm majoring in business, playing polo and fighting in sham battles. What else could I want?" Kit ushered him to his table. "Say hi to Mom and Dad. And this young lady is Mary Lou Folkner, my date for the Atlantic City weekend."

Jack greeted them all, directing a little more attention toward Mary Lou, who looked very grown up and especially pretty.

They made small talk about the time at Lewes, the jelly fish and the hammerhead shark. As the waitress brought dessert, Jack excused himself, saying he had to return to his friends at his table.

Gerry and Phil drove back to the hotel. Kit and Mary Lou elected to walk the boardwalk back. The half moon was over the ocean offering a proud reflection, warming their affections for each other. Hand in hand, their shoulders touched willingly as they strolled on contentedly. They arrived at the hotel and took the elevator up to the suite she was sharing with Gerry and Phil. Before they went in, Kit took her in his arms and kissed her. Mary Lou put her arms around his neck and moved as close to him as possible. They both felt the passionate stimulation brought on by the warmth of the kiss.

When they finally broke it off, Kit said, "That was a great beginning of something more than our long friendship. Sorry to end it, but I must say goodnight to Mom and Dad. I'm due back at my own room."

Mary Lou gave him a quick kiss on the cheek before they went in.

Kit's drill for Sunday was to leave Atlantic City at 10:00 A.M. with the Corps and return to WMA. They planned to meet for breakfast in the hotel dining room at 8:00 A.M., and then go on their way.

By the time they got to breakfast, Kit and Mary Lou were anxious to see each other. They were both smitten, wishing they had more time together, alone. They made the best of what was given them.

When the time came, Kit helped them load the car. He and Mary Lou looked at each other longingly, hoping it would not be too long until they were together again.

Chapter XVIII

As the school year went on, Kit found academically he was in good shape. In addition to the required business curriculum, military science was also required. This, along with his infantry and cavalry training, gave him an inherent pride like one that wells from within when watching a marching band playing the Star Spangled Banner.

The administration had designed a complete academic program, including social activities and religious services along with the ordinary requirements.

The social activities included the popular Copper Beech Ball, named for the huge copper beech tree standing proudly in front of "Old Main." The Ball, an established tradition, was the next scheduled activity.

Freddie and Kit were filled with anticipation. Freddie invited a striking brunette whom he'd met at his tennis club at home. Called Margie by close friends, her name was Marge Shey.

Mary Lou was in dreamland since Kit invited her. She hoped she had finally turned Kit's head.

The night they had all waited for arrived. The girls' families provided transportation to the ball and the cadets met them as they arrived.

When Mr. Folkner delivered Mary Lou, Kit was waiting for her in his dress uniform. As Mary Lou got out of the car, she took his breath. She looked fully matured in her beautiful black evening gown. He took her hand and then handed her a corsage of gardenias.

Kit greeted Mr. Folkner thanking him for bringing Mary Lou. As Kit and Mary Lou walked toward the Armory he said, "You look beautiful. I have been anxious all day for you to arrive. It's been worth waiting for."

She said, "I prepared most of the afternoon. My, how handsome you are in your dress uniform."

They entered the armory, greeting those they both knew, and Kit introduced her to other friends she had not met. They drifted over toward the receiving line where they were announced to the president and his wife and other official administrators and faculty members.

The president held a colonel's commission which he held in high esteem. He was a fine equestrian and had a sincere love of horses. This, in part, supported his decision to have a polo team. Very few colleges opted for polo as it was a loser financially.

The Battalion Captain and his date started the first dance with everyone else joining in quickly.

As the evening wore on, Al Tyler planned to irritate Kit by leering at Mary Lou whenever the opportunity presented itself. Tyler's date had excused herself, and he was standing alone just off the dance area as Kit and Mary Lou danced by. He commented loud enough for both of them to hear, "Hey Fox, I'll bet you she's a hot number in the back seat."

Kit ignored his remark and kept on dancing which rather surprised Mary Lou. When they finished their dance, he asked her to wait by the refreshment table. He had never taken his eyes from Tyler. He walked over to him, "Tyler, if you've got any guts at all, I'll meet you behind the observatory at 8:00 o'clock Monday night."

"I'll be waiting for you. Tell your date, when she wants a man to look me up."

Kit let it go and went back to Mary Lou.

At the intermission, Kit got Mary Lou's wrap; they were stepping out for a stroll and some fresh air. As they wandered over behind the stadium holding hands, she asked, "Is he always that crass or does he have a chip on his shoulder about something?"

"He and I are competing for the last position on the polo team. He's obviously provoking me into a showdown."

"What's that supposed to mean?"

"I was offended by his insult of you and gave him an ultimatum which he accepted."

"Ouch. Tell me!"

"To meet him behind the observatory."

"Do you think it a wise decision? What is the administration's feeling on fighting?"

"I really don't know. I've been told that when the dispute gets this serious it should be settled in the gym. I never thought of the gym when I said the observatory."

"I know whatever I say won't change your mind as you feel my reputation insult is going unanswered and undefended. I appreciate your concern but in no way do I want you to jeopardize your career here."

"I'll not back down, you mean too much and he can't be left unchallenged. Don't worry, my career won't be affected," Kit took her in his arms and kissed her, feeling a tremendous emotion from her body pressing against him. The kiss became more sensual triggering his desire to make love to her. When she broke off the kiss, they remained in the embrace breathing heavily.

She said, "We'd better get back. I'm sure the intermission is over."

He thought the intermission be damned.

They danced the evening away relishing each others company.

When the activities were over, the dates who had travelled some distance had special overnight arrangements. Mary Lou's father was picking her up. They tried to steal a few kisses as they walked across the campus to meet Mr. Folkner, but met with little success. They spotted the Folkner car, and as Kit opened the door, Freddie Burner and his date walked by. Freddie said, "Tyler asked me to tell you he is looking forward to your meeting Monday night. You can tell me what it's all about later."

Mary Lou rolled her eyes and got in the car saying goodnight.

On Monday night, Kit was finishing up an English assignment, it was just 7:30 and he changed into his sweat suit. Learning of the incident and where Kit was meeting Tyler, Freddie wanted to go too, but Kit said "No!" The fewer people that knew, the better.

Kit arrived at the observatory five minutes early. Fortunately, no one was in the area. At five minutes past eight, nothing. Suddenly, he was grabbed around the neck from the back. Tyler had sneaked up behind him, to take him by surprise. Kit tried to pry up the strong arms wrapped around his neck. He was having trouble breathing, as he couldn't budge the arms. Tyler tried to throw him down on the ground, but Kit had his feet planted wide apart. Kit grabbed the arms making sure they didn't loosen, then he bent forward as far and quickly as he could, sending Tyler over him, breaking his hold. Tyler landed on his back but rolled over and scrambled to his feet. They squared off, sparring looking for an opening. Kit feigned a jab to the stomach, Tyler dropped his guard and Kit landed a powerful right to his jaw knocking him back; he followed up with a left to the mouth. Tyler decided to take Kit down with a tackle. He did and scrambled on top of him swinging a right hand that caught Kit's nose. Kit got his right hand under Tyler's chin and pushed up as hard as he could and rolled over on Tyler's leg, pinning it and pulling him off him. Both started to get up and Kit swung from the ground, landing a right under Tyler's chin sending him sprawling on the ground. He went over to him and as he started to get up, he hit Tyler again dropping him back to his knees. Tyler shook his head, Kit backed off. Tyler got up and kicked out at Kit, he caught his foot with his hands and gave it a quick twist throwing Tyler off balance, as he fell, Kit jumped on him pinning him to the ground. He said, "You're a yellow coward, attacking me from the rear. I should beat you within an inch of your life. Don't ever insult a girl I'm with again."

Tyler's face was covered with blood. Kit decided he'd given him enough. He got up, leaving Tyler on the ground. Both were covered with grass stain and dirt. Tyler felt he'd been hit by a truck; he stayed on the ground trying to collect himself as Kit walked back to "Old Main."

Chapter XIX

The holiday season in full swing, the cadets were ready for their Christmas furlough. Several cadets from Cuba were invited to spend the holidays in the States at homes of their classmates. Pancho Lopez had befriended Kit and happily agreed to a furlough with Kit and his family.

Pancho's family home was in Havana. His father was in Batista's cabinet and was a close friend of the Cuban leader. The family was one of the select families that had position and wealth along with privileges afforded the leader's friends. Cuba's luxurious resort hotels on its beautiful beaches lured tourists from the U.S. and other countries. Its economy was supported by tourism, cigars, sugar and rum. For the most part, the people were either rich or poor, the poor vastly outnumbering the wealthy.

Batista relied on the military to sustain his power and position among his people. Any uprising was quickly quelled. On the beautiful island, politics and the military were dependant on one another. The affluent families, preparing their sons for government positions, sent them to military colleges in the States for officer training and academic proficiency.

Pancho's beautiful mother had striking light brown eyes set off by long dark lashes and black hair. Standing at five feet, five inches, her attractive figure drew both brazen and discreet stares from men. His sister was two years younger than he and starting to bloom in the right places, showing promise of looking very much like her mother.

Pancho was a very handsome young man, standing an even six feet with dark hair and kind blue eyes, olive skin and a rugged image. His temperament was even and well controlled.

Mr. Lopez was the Minister of Defense and felt the importance of a strong military presence in the overall scheme of a properly run government. A man of strong character and intelligence, he was short, and solid, and impressive in his uniform, with piercing blue eyes and black hair sprinkled with grey.

With his position and background, he influenced Pancho to attend a military college. Being brought up in a military atmosphere, Pancho always seriously considered a military career.

The family's wealth came from real estate holdings along with the minister's remuneration from his government position. Mr. Lopez carefully guided his son, preparing him for the fortunes and misfortunes of life, making certain he would not be spoiled by wealth and social standing. Pancho worked his summers laboring in construction crews, building the Lopez real estate empire and in maintenance crews keeping the existing buildings in good repair. This plan worked and Pancho quickly learned the values of hard labor and what it takes to achieve life's financial treasures.

Several Cubans were already attending Waterville Military Academy. Mr. Lopez learned of the college through the parents of these students. They strongly recommended it. Determined to check further, he wrote to the president, a Colonel Henry Wyatt, requesting the college military and academic curricula. The response convinced him to send Pancho to the Chester college when he finished his preparatory schooling.

When Pancho arrived at WMA, he and Kit hit it off quite well from the start. Both had a keen interest in the military and specifically the cavalry. They both rode hard on bivouacs, enjoying every moment.

Having become good friends, it was quite natural that Kit invited him to spend his furlough at Fox Lair.

Gerry was at "Old Main" when their furlough commenced. They anxiously greeted him and then piled into the car. As they drove up to Fox Lair, Kit realized he had missed his family and home. Phil came out the kitchen door as they drove around to the rear of the house. Kit jumped out of the car, ran to his mother, embraced her and lifted her off the ground. She said, "You've taken my breath away, but I love it. Let me welcome Pancho."

Pancho called to her, "I've been anxiously waiting to meet you," walking over to embrace her. "Your hacienda is beautiful, I'm honored to be here and hope it's not too much trouble."

"It's no trouble at all, you fit right in like one of the family," she smiled warmly leading him toward the house.

As they all went inside, the snow commenced to fall.

Mary Lou made her appearance at mid-afternoon. Kit walked over and gave her a hug as she walked into the living room. He stood back, taking her in. She had grown more beautiful and filled out perfectly in the short time since he had last seen her. Pancho then went over and greeted her, "How's the beautiful neighbor?"

"I'm fine thank you. Señor, wait till you meet the date I've arranged for you on Christmas Eve. You'll be glad you came to visit," she winked at him.

"Why can't I meet her sooner, this senorita? I'm anxious to know her name," he smiled, nodding his head.

"First of all, she's a freshman at Slippery Rock and she's not home from college yet. However, her name is Hedy Dumas and she lives out in West Chester, maybe eight miles from here. We met during summer tennis competition. She has a great serve and covers a lot of ground on the court. She said she'd call me when she arrives home, and we'll see what we can arrange."

"I'll cool my heels while I'm waiting."

Phil suggested they have some coffee or tea and cookies she just baked. They went out to the big country kitchen and found seats around the large oak table with hand-carved, clawed feet and legs. They listened to the exploits of the two cadets laughing about the jackass that pulled the cannon on bivouac: he sat down and wouldn't move; finally, when he did get up, he went backwards instead of forward. He pushed the cannon into a ditch off the side of the road, where it got stuck. By the time they got the cannon free, the jackass had fallen asleep. When he was awakened, he was more stubborn than ever. The senior officers decided to confiscate Pancho's horse to pull the cannon and have Pancho ride the jackass. He saddled him and mounted, he goaded, spurred, coaxed and swore as the jackass would take three steps forward and four steps back. Eventually, he got him to trot. He wouldn't do anything else, no gallop, no walk, just trot. By the time they got back to camp Pancho felt the ache in every bone in his body. Two hours of constant trotting almost did him in, and the jackass almost killed himself through utter exhaustion. After an hour of catching up, Kit, Mary Lou and Pancho went horseback riding through the countryside.

The Folkners invited everyone next door for dinner at seven. Both families were compatible, making Mary Lou's family and Kit's relationship very comfortable.

Pancho turned out to be the hit of the evening. With a great deal of presence, he thrived on center stage. With his striking good looks and innate intelligence, he held their attention with entertaining stories about Cuba.

In the course of the evening, Hedy phoned as soon as she arrived home asking if they could join forces tomorrow at her home so that she and Pancho could meet.

Saturday afternoon found Kit, Mary Lou and Pancho driving out to West Chester, that charming town where West Chester State Teacher's College proudly educated future educators. Old Main, a large multi-story structure, was built of serpentine stone, indigenous to this area of Chester County. The college was also a rival of WMA's football team.

Hedy lived on the outskirts of town on the Wilmington-West Chester Pike in an attractive Pennsylvania farmhouse, circa 1853, on some 32 acres. She was helping her mother prepare sand tarts in their spacious kitchen as the three visitors arrived. The aroma in the house welcomed them along with Hedy. Mary Lou looked at Pancho as she made the introductions. His look reflected his keen interest. Hedy was a striking, blond-haired, blue-eyed seventeen year old with all the endowments attractively proportioned. Hedy, likewise, was taken with Pancho's charm and handsomeness, creating an air of magnetism between them.

She welcomed them, directing her attention to Pancho. "We are fortunate you chose WMA, otherwise we may not have met."

"Hedy, it's fate, I feel we were destined to meet."

"Please come to the kitchen to meet my mother."

"If she is responsible for the aroma that's teasing us, I can barely wait."

Mrs. Dumas was a tall, forty-year old with a warm exuberance present in her beautiful face. Not only did mother and daughter resemble one another, they obviously had that respect and love shared by mother and daughter under an ideal relationship. After the introductions, she passed the delicious cookies to the guests.

Their plans were to have dinner back at Kit's and either stay in or go to a neighborhood party. During dinner it started to snow again, so they decided to stay put.

Gerry had built a large knotty pine panelled recreation room in the basement, with a large wet bar, backed by a large mirror and indirect lighting, cafe tables and chairs, a pool table, a nickelodeon and an area to dance.

After dinner, the young folks excused themselves and adjourned to the rec room. Had anyone observed during dinner, they would have noticed the eye communication between Hedy and Pancho. Now that they were away from the scrutiny of Kit's Mom and Dad, Pancho said, "Kit, if you would play the music box, I would ask Hedy to dance."

"How about *Right at Home*? It's perfect for dancing."

"A great idea, assuming Hedy will join me for a dance," he commented, looking at her hopefully.

"If that's an invitation, I will if you promise to behave yourself," she teased.

"I hope you don't inhibit me before I even dance with you."

They started to dance, moved by Ibach's rich piano solo. Pancho was delighted the way Hedy put her left arm up around his neck and put her cheek to his, dancing ever so closely. Hedy became emotional as they spun around the floor, she partly stradled his pivoting leg. They danced the night away, drinking cokes and sharing a cigarette occasionally.

Mary Lou and Kit found a secluded area back by the heater room so that they could have some privacy, leaving Hedy and Pancho dancing alone. Pancho eventually realized this, and thought what a perfect time to steal a kiss.

Pancho stopped dancing and gently took her chin in his thumb and forefinger, raising her head. "I've had the strongest desire to kiss your beautiful lips." With that, he kissed her fully and she responded by parting her lips. Breathing heavily, her body warmed up to him in a sexual rhythmic motion. Being a hot blooded Cuban, Pancho got so excited he almost lost control. Eventually, he was the one who broke it off, concerned that Kit and Mary Lou might bounce in while he was trying to compose himself.

Hedy said, "Well Señor, it seems we have fun together. My engine was just starting to purr. Discretion has reared its ugly head only to short-circuit a memorable experience."

The timing was right, Kit and Mary Lou came back into the room.

Pancho said quietly, "Just in the nick of time. Had we continued it could have been embarrassing. I know you're going home early tomorrow, but can't we spend some time together next week?" Hedy nodded in agreement.

Hedy's father was a partner in a mushroom business. He also tried to keep a protective eye on his beautiful daughter, suspecting every healthy young man she knew of having lascivious designs on her.

During the holiday week, the two couples spent as much time together as possible. When they were at Hedy's house, Mr. Dumas watched Pancho like a mama bear watching her cub. As a consequence, with Hedy feeling a bit frisky, she preferred they spend their time elsewhere.

One of the holiday evenings Gerry and Phil were out at a neighbor's party which created the opportunity the young lovers were waiting for. Kit and Mary Lou were very casual about their love, outwardly they were very private. Whatever they did was guarded. On the other hand, Hedy and Pancho were explosive, seeming to embrace at a moment's notice. Kit and Mary Lou wandered off to find some seclusion while Pancho and Hedy were seated on the sofa in the living room. Pancho dimmed the lights and in no time they were in a heated embrace. His first move after some preliminary kissing, was to reach up under her sweater and wrestle with her bra. Neither was experienced, and their legs got intertwined with shifting and pumping, Hedy's skirt worked up to her thighs.

Pancho said, "Won't you slip your panties off?" She worked them down over her knees with one hand then did the rest with her legs and feet. By some good fortune they managed to fulfill their mission. Hedy had her legs still wrapped around Pancho and continued to stay in that position; he couldn't get up.

After several minutes he said, "This position is great for making love, but a little uncomfortable for any permanence. Do you think you could release me from this dead lock position?"

She laughed, "I would but my pants never got over my right shoe and they're hooked on the wooden knob on the sofa arm rest."

Mr. Dumas' concern was not wasted.

As the holidays rolled to a close, Pancho and Hedy bid a reluctant farewell with promises of seeing each other at Spring break.

Chapter XX

1933-34

Kit's relationship with Mary Lou had strengthened. They were on a path leading to marriage. Neither had eyes for anyone else. At WMA he was an upper classman due to graduate. Academically, he was still doing well, ranking in the top 10 percentile. His military training was second nature to him; he liked everything about it: the cavalry, the ordnance, the military science and tactics. Summer camp and maneuvers were a treat rather than a treatment. As he excelled in the military, he became battalion captain. He loved the dress parades. The entire corps in cadence, responding perfectly to parade commands, all to the rhythm of the marches played by the band.

The polo team developed into a contender for the national indoor championship. Although Princeton won the cup in '32 and Yale in '33, each team lost valuable players through graduation. WMA, with the same starting team this year as last, expected great things of themselves. The starters were Kit, Harvey Beels, Joe McKee and Al Tyler.

Kit and Beels had become very close. They teamed well, knowing what to expect from the other during a match. Beels walked over to Kit after practice, "You know Kit, if we have a weak link on this team it's Tyler. He thinks more of himself than the team. Many times he forces a shot instead of passing off, as it were, to one of us who's open. We could be scoring more goals."

"Harvey, why don't you talk to him? You might make him think more of team play. He won't listen to me as we barely tolerate each other."

Beels went over to Tyler, "Al, we're a strong contender for the national title this year. Our position would improve if you would pass up some of those forced shots you take. Most of the time one of us is usually open with a much better chance at a goal."

Tyler got an irritated look as he responded, "I'm the best shot; that's why I take them. Did that wimp Fox put you up to this? I can ride circles around him any time."

"The truth of the matter is, few can ride circles around Kit, especially when he's on Win. He's got the highest goal rating on the team, five I think."

"You're another one, both of you only take shots when they're easy," Tyler stood looking at him challenging.

Beels, eye-to-eye, answered, "It takes good riders to position themselves to get easy shots. I heard somewhere that that was the name of the game: score goals. In any event, it wasn't my purpose to argue. I just wanted to get your cooperation on sharing the ball."

Tyler spoke over his shoulder as he walked away, "I'll think about it, but don't hold your breath."

CHAPTER XXI

Thursday night, Jake, the beloved groom, made his last round in the riding hall and stables. With the Princeton match on Saturday, he was anxious for all things to be in order. Finishing the riding hall, he went on to the stables. At each stall he greeted the pony by name, sharing a few kind words along the way. From a distance, it appeared something was askew down the line. When he approached the last three stalls, he discovered they were empty: three of their best ponies gone, the three stall doors were ajar.

He searched the stable and the grounds looking for clues or evidence as to where they might be, and who took them. The search produced nothing. He knew the drill - notify the Commandant of any emergency regardless of the hour. It was 11:14 P.M.

The Commandant was a Colonel Winston Whistlebottom. He'd earned his spurs in the cavalry in World War I. Enlisted as a private, he worked his way to staff sergeant and won a second lieutenant's field commission for extraordinary tactical ability and valor in the battle at Verdun. When he became a bird colonel, he was assigned to WMA as the Commandant of the Corps of Cadets.

Colonel Whistlebottom enjoyed the gracious liberties extended him by the dietitian in the absence of his wife, who happened to be spending a week visiting her parents. The dietitian, Gretel, was pretty, plump and from Intercourse in the beautiful farmlands of the Pennsylvania Dutch country. She was so magnificently endowed, the cadets did a right face, a left face or an about face when she was within sight, just to see her bounce as she wiggle waggled down the aisles of the mess hall.

She and the Colonel were what the Cadets called "objective secured." Moaning and groaning, Gretel was frowning, biting her lower lip and Whistlebottom was frantically banging away with a huff and a puff.

There was a loud rap on the front door.

"Now what ungodly soul would interrupt this moment sent from heaven? If I don't answer, perhaps whoever it is will go away."

"Colonel, I don't want to get caught here," still continuing her sexual duties, "But I would like to finish what we've started."

The rapping became louder.

The Colonel reluctantly slowed down and Gretel released her scissors grip. He swore as he rolled off and got up. He slipped on his robe and slippers then turned to her saying, "Stay put, I'll only be a minute."

Whistlebottom descended the staircase. Whoever it was, he didn't want to let in. He called through the door, "Who is it? What do you want?"

"It's me, Jake, Colonel. Please open up."

He cracked the door and Jake blurted out, "Three of our best ponies'er missin'. Come quick."

"You go back to the stable and I'll be along directly," wanting to get back upstairs, he asked no further questions.

Meanwhile, when Gretel heard the voices downstairs, she partly panicked: she jumped out of bed, turned the light out and hid in the clothes closet.

The Colonel ran up the stairs anxious to finish his business. He came out of his slippers, threw off his robe and jumped into bed saying, "Let's finish it up." He leaned over and kissed her with his lips parted. He got the funny feeling he'd kissed a runny nose and the hair on her head. He reached for the light on the night table, switching it on. "What kind of a kiss was that?"

Just then Gretel emerged from the closet. She looked at the bed exclaiming, "What's your mutt doing in my spot?"

"He must have jumped in when you got out. My God, I kissed the dog right on his snout!" He spit and wiped his mouth.

"He apparently enjoyed it, he's looking at you with that affectionate look in his eyes."

"Don't be silly; he's bewildered, it never happened to him before. I guess we'd better call it a night. I have to report down to the stables."

Getting dressed, Gretel said laughingly, "First me, then the mutt and now the ponies, eh? I'll slip out the back door, love."

Chapter XXII

Whistlebottom arrived at the stables just behind Jake wondering why the ponies were gone. Strangely enough, no one admitted hearing anything when they disappeared. With no evidence and being inhibited by the darkness, the Colonel ordered the area secured. The investigation would continue in the morning.

Bright and early, the Colonel was at the stables searching the entire area finding very little aside from some hoof prints that were unidentifiable. The detective, Graham, wondered how they knew to take the three best ponies, prompting a comment to Whistlebottom that he suspected it was an inside job.

Without the top ponies, WMA would be at a definite disadvantage against Princeton. They needed the win in their quest for the national championship.

Kit learned of the horsenapping through the grapevine. His first free moment found him looking for Jake whom he found in the stables. In answer to his questions, he learned Jake found them missing shortly after 11:00 P.M. and that there was no new evidence. He told Jake he was anxious to help in anyway at all.

On Saturday morning Princeton arrived for the important match. The winner would be in undisputed first place in the league.

Harvey, Joe, Tyler and Kit met privately after the team meeting. Harvey said, "Let's not take the risky shots. Wait for the proper opening or pass-off to someone with better position and a chance for a clear shot." Quiet Joe McKee spoke up unexpectedly, "Al, today you should pass off instead of taking those high risk shots."

Tyler looked at the other three, "Is Fox putting you up to this stupid criticism? I'm the mallet man on the team; I have a good chance of making those shots."

"Fox didn't put us up to anything, even the spectators can see your bad shots. Most of the time one of us has better position; look around before you shoot, see where we are," Joe replied.

"Get off my back, I'm the reason we're where we are. I'm playing my own game," Tyler wasn't backing down.

"We would be alone in first place if you hadn't missed all those crazy shots. You're a first team player, but you grandstand too much. For God's sake, why are you so obstinate? Harvey, Kit and I aren't all wrong. Cooperate!"

Going into the final chukker the score was tied at two apiece. Tyler possessed the ball, a Princeton rider was riding to cut him off. Kit galloped toward the goal positioned for a good shot. Tyler looked over at him and then fired his own shot from a ridiculous angle. Blocked by the opposition, his shot missed widely. Princeton, with possession of the ball, worked toward its goal. Kit on Win, made a brilliant move, stealing the ball knocking it over to Harvey, who then galloped toward the WMA goal exhibiting his outstanding polo expertise, feinting and outdistancing the Princeton players. There was one between him and the goal. Spotting Joe McKee positioned for a perfect shot, he knocked him the ball, and Joe put it away with a perfect shot between the goals. Their lead held and WMA won three to two. The win was somewhat unexpected as they'd played without their three best ponies.

Jake met them as they brought their ponies back to the stable. He was so proud of the riders and the ponies, he was near tears knowing what this win meant.

The players savored the win. Kit, Joe and Harvey each scored a goal with Tyler recording a goose egg. He had taken more shots, all reckless and forced; his ego larger than ever even though he'd come up empty. "Hey Fox," he called, "did you notice I outplayed you on defense? I really rode those Princetonians off from the goal."

"You were simply doing what we all did, but your scoring technique needs work. Why don't you trot right out now and practice?

Incidentally, what do you think of the horsenapping, Tyler?"

"I'm baffled by it, but I'd like to catch whoever did it; I'd beat up on them."

"That's the first thing you and I have agreed on."

"Don't jump to conclusions Fox. I was thinking maybe you had something to do with it."

"Looks like I did jump. You're a real piece of work. I pity the poor slob that gets stuck with you; she'd better be prepared for a lifetime with Mr. Snake Pit. Now, pardon me, I'm going to get some air that doesn't reek of your putrefaction."

Kit met Pancho going back to his room. He greeted him, "Buenos dias, Amigo."

"Your Spanish is improving. I'm fine thank you. Everyone is talking about the missing ponies. Is there anything new?"

"Nothing that I've heard. Say, Pancho, some of the boys are talking of a short cruise Sunday on the Wilson Line. It should be fun. Why don't you join us?"

"With dates?"

"No, just the boys."

Chapter XXIII

In close proximity to the College, was a neighborhood nicknamed Frog Pond. Other city neighborhoods also carried nicknames: Holy City near St. Michael's Church; the West End (which was the southern end of town); Waterville, a small group of homes near Ridley Creek, Sun Village, Sun Hill and Buckman Village.

Frog Ponders were mostly families of meager means, proud of their Frog Pond heritage. Their homes were modest brick rows and twins with spotty maple trees in the front or rear yards, some along the streets. The sidewalks were original worn brick. Along with the homes were a few small businesses where these folks worked. Some baked and delivered the tastiest of baked bread and rolls at Dalton's Bakery. Others worked at Crystle's Dairy where the milk and cream were separated and bottled then loaded on milk trucks for home delivery. *The Frog Pond* was a popular taproom where the customers enjoyed wine and beer mixed with spirited dialogue. A famous landmark in Frog Pond was the Goodwill Firehouse where every able-bodied male was a member. When the siren went off, all available men went running out their front doors, donning jackets and hats; others already in the ready room would hit the pole for immediate descent from the second floor to the first; then, with sirens blaring, the fire trucks wheeled out racing toward the fire with the likes of Murph Buffano, the best driver in the City, at the wheel.

Wild Dog, an old buddy of Gerry's, lived in Frog Pond; he worked at Dalton's Bakery, stopped in *The Frog Pond* to swill an occasional beer and was a member of Goodwill as they called it. As did all Frog Ponders, he had a devoted interest in WMA and all its activities.

Wild Dog and his wife Matilda had two sons: the older big, the younger not so big. Because they cracked the other kid heads, they were nicknamed Big and Little Cracker. Growing up, they spent much of their leisure time at WMA, and more particularly around the stables, hoping for odd jobs and bothering Jake for his blessings. He doled out what few jobs there were. Entering their teens, both dropped out of school; first Big and then Little. Not making the grades in school, in life they were proud of the grade they were receiving, an "I" - for Incorrigible.

Taking to gambling, Big and Little Cracker started conducting crap games in an alley off Parker Street beside the High School. Ten or twelve kids usually joined the game at lunchtime or after school. As the dice rolled, they cut the pot from time to time often picking up ten or twelve dollars a day. At night and on Saturdays, they won handily at the local pool hall below the Roberta Apartments on Seventh Street downtown.

As their reputation grew, the brothers were contacted by a gambling syndicate. The syndicate had heavy gamblers looking for the opportunity to try a different game of chance. Briefed on the plan the brothers agreed to participate.

The gambling event took place, but the plan backfired with the syndicate taking a heavy hit. Big and Little Cracker were paid for their efforts. Deciding it was time for some entertainment, they planned a Wilson Line excursion on Sunday.

Chapter XXIV

Upon her return, Colonel Whistlebottom's wife Agnes, sensed something unnatural about her bedroom. A sense women possess. She couldn't pinpoint the reason for the nagging feeling, but it was there. She couldn't accuse Winston of misconduct because of intuition. Because she was upset, she was unconsciously difficult with him.

Already guilt ridden, Whistlebottom was confused by her attitude. He went to the bedroom, checking for telltale evidence left by Gretel. He found nothing. Could anyone have seen her leaving? Jake. That must have been it and somehow Agnes had learned of his indiscretion.

Thinking about Jake, he wondered - no definitely not - Jake wouldn't have had anything to do with the missing ponies. But if he knew of the Colonel and Gretel, maybe he should get rid of him. Jake was loved by the cadets, the professors, the administration, everyone. The Colonel's imagination started to churn. As of yet, there were no suspects, and Jake was the one who made the discovery. A case might be made that he released the ponies and then reported them missing to cover up.

He devised his plan to suggest his suspicion to several people; they would relate to others, laying the ground work. He would then confront Jake with the accusation.

Gretel was the most important of his contacts. She should be as interested in Jakes's removal as he was. He waited until she was at loose ends in the kitchen before approaching her, saying, "Agnes senses something went on when she was visiting her parents. Jake probably saw you leave that night and put two and two together.

Somehow Agnes has gotten wind of it. If I can get Jake dismissed because of an involvement in the pony theft, our problem might disappear."

"No one will believe Jake would be involved in that mess. He loves the ponies, the polo team and the Cadets."

"I know that. But if you spread the word you can leave the rest to me. I have a few others I can count on to cooperate and help put the plan to work," he urged.

"Okay, I'll give it a try," she responded, turning her attention to her clipboard.

The word spread and, while most felt it was incredulous, there was no one else under suspicion.

The rumor eventually got to Jake. Jake was an honest, loving person who never hurt anyone unless provoked unreasonably. That his integrity was questioned was a terrible blow. Outwardly, he kept a stiff upper lip; inwardly, his heart was breaking.

Kit ran into Jake at the stable and saw the distress in his eyes. He tried to help, "Jake, the Cadets know you aren't involved in this situation. Someone started the rumor, hoping to pin it on you."

"The last thing I would ever do is anything to hurt those ponies. They are like my own. I'm at a loss figuring out who started this. If worse comes to worse, and I lose my job, it would break my heart, I love it here." With that said, Kit looked at him and saw the tears well up in his eyes.

"Jake, I can't guarantee anything but most of the corps is behind you," he gave him a reassuring pat on the shoulder.

The next day, Whistlebottom wandered down to the stables to confront Jake. He found him brushing down one of the ponies, "Jake, come out here, I want to talk to you."

"Colonel, I swear I had nothin' to do with that. I love this place and everything about it. I'd never do anything to damage it. Where does this rumor come from? Who told ya?"

"I can't tell you who told me. But with this rumor circulating, I'm afraid I must suspend you until your involvement can be determined."

"What involvement? I've done nothing wrong. How can you suspend me for something I haven't done? I have a perfect record with the college. If you're suspending me, I'll go to Colonel Wyatt. He's known me for years."

"Now hold on, Jake, let me rethink this a moment. I'll reserve my judgment on the suspension for a day or two. But don't get too settled; things don't look good."

"Colonel, I don't know who started this vicious rumor or why, but he is wrong," his distress was clear in the frown.

Jake turned and went back to his grooming. He couldn't understand why the Colonel didn't believe him.

The Colonel knew he had to keep the rumor alive to accomplish his plan. If too much time passed, the real culprits could surface and Jake would remain on campus as a nemesis.

Chapter XXV

Coincidentally, Kit, Pancho and several other Cadets and Big and Little Cracker were waiting for the Wilson Line on the pier at the end of Market Street at the Delaware River.

When the graceful excursion liner docked, all the anxious passengers boarded, positioning themselves to view the sights along the way - the industry along the shoreline, the tankers and freighters passing in the river. They either stood by the railing or sat back in deck chairs enjoying the cruise down to the next port of call, Riverview Beach.

All the passengers went ashore. The kids ran to the merry-go-round and the bumper cars. The Cadets got hot dogs and sodas to take to the picnic grounds. After they finished eating, they took a ride on the roller coaster and walked the park, eyeing the young ladies.

Aboard ship once again, they strolled the decks, listened to the orchestra, talked to the girls they met and danced occasionally. At the stern of the ship, Kit heard a ruckus.

The Cracker boys had some booze and were drunk and loud. Big Cracker yelled out, "Hey Little, let's turn the heat up and start cracking around."

Little Cracker spotted Kit and Pancho as they arrived at the scene. "Yo, tin soldiers, what'cha doin' aboard ship, ain't you out of your element?"

"You might say we're enjoying the excursion," Pancho replied.

"Ain't you one of them polo players?"

Kit looked at Little, "I play a bit, why?"

"How'd ya win the Princeton match?" Taking a swig from his bottle, he added, "Three of your ponies was snatched."

Kit sensed an opportunity, "What do you know about the missing ponies?"

In a drunken lunge, Big pushed Kit saying, "What's it to you?"

Kit ignored the shove, "We need those ponies. Where are they?"

"You'll never know, sucker. You should have lost to Princeton. You made some important people teed off winning that one," Big Cracker's eyes were glassy, and his breath reeked of Green River.

"You stole them didn't you? I remember you two guys. Big and Little Cracker, sons of my Dad's old friend Wild Dog. If you fess up and return the ponies, maybe the college won't prefer charges."

"You must be crazy, we're not admittin' anything. Everyone knows the ponies are missin'. Why don't you get lost before I crack you around?" Big yelled in Kit's face.

"You tempt me, Cracker. Believe me, when I'm out of WMA, I'll give it a go with you. I can't wait."

"I'm ready now. Are you yellow?" Big swayed backwards as he spoke.

"We'll get it on in due time, and you'll see how yellow I am."

With that, they went their separate ways. "I was aching to take a poke at him, but if I were caught fighting, I'd get thrown out of school," Kit admitted.

Anxious to clear Jake, Kit went in search of Colonel Whistlebottom as soon as he returned to the campus. He finally found him in the mess hall talking to Gretel. The Colonel noticed him standing off to the side waiting. "Yes, Fox, what is it?"

"If I could speak to you privately, Sir?"

"Wait outside, I'll be with you in a minute."

Kit stepped outside, the Colonel followed shortly. "Okay, what now?"

Kit related his experiences on the Wilson Line with the Crackers. "I know it's not conclusive evidence, but they did say some people were upset because we didn't lose to Princeton. Doesn't that smell of some kind of gambling involvement?"

The Colonel wanted to keep the heat on Jake, and he didn't like Kit's new information. "I think you're grabbing at straws; there's nothing concrete in your discovery. Leave it with me. And don't spread it around until I check it out."

As Kit left the Colonel, he began to wonder who else might have been involved. He was sure Jake was innocent. Who could the Crackers have gotten to cooperate? Someone who knew the ponies could keep them quiet when released from their stalls. Because of his dislike for Tyler, he wondered if he could have been involved. He had a penchant toward risk and gambling as demonstrated by his polo antics. He would keep his eyes and ears open to learn what he could. Kit also wondered why the Colonel lacked enthusiasm about the Crackers.

The Colonel was feeling anxiety. He had to move if he was to get rid of Jake. The Cracker information was pushing him.

His plan took him to the President's office, where he waited until Colonel Wyatt could work him into his busy schedule. The secretary offered him a seat and a copy of Liberty magazine to calm his impatience. Eventually, the secretary beckoned him to follow her to the office door; Colonel Wyatt offered him his hand in a gesture of friendship. Whistlebottom shook it vigorously, and Wyatt recovered his hand as quickly as possible, he hated the exaggerated pumping motion. "Yes, Whistlebottom, what news have you regarding the missing ponies?"

"Well, Sir, there's a rumor circulating regarding two boys from Frog Pond. Seems they've been shooting off a bit about the incident. Cadet Fox had an encounter with them and thinks there might be more to it than there appears: some gambling motivation. In any event there had to be some inside cooperation, some one who knew the ponies - to keep the noise down. It must've been Jake."

"Why do you feel so strongly it was Jake?"

Whistlebottom hated the question. "Sir, he's the logical one." His mind worked quickly. If there was gambling involved, there was a pay-off. "Jake's grandson has medical problems. His scarlet fever left him with a heart condition and the family's hard pressed to meet the medical expenses."

Wyatt grudgingly agreed in his own mind to talk to Jake. "Send Jake up to see me. I want to have a chat with him."

Whistlebottom started to get a feeling of relief. Jake may be dismissed and with that his problems with Agnes might be eased. He went to the stables and found Jake in his office sitting dejectedly, looking out the window.

"Jake, Colonel Wyatt wants to see you. Would you go up to his office on the double?"

Jake didn't answer, he simply got up from his desk and left the office. Walking up the long walk to "Old Main," his head hanging low, he wondered, what will I ever do if I'm let go? My name would be disgraced, no one would hire me. I'm being framed!

But why? I've never hurt anybody.

When he arrived, the Colonel's secretary showed him in. "Jake, come on in and have a seat. It's time we had a chat."

As Jake sat, he said, "Yes Sir, thank you."

"Jake, there's some word around on campus involving you with the missing ponies. Something about you're needing money to help with medical expenses for your grandson."

"Colonel, I'd never meddle with those ponies. I love WMA, I love the Cadets, I love the ponies. Why did someone start this rumor? Do you know who thinks it was me?"

"Jake, I'm not able to disclose that now," he thought for a moment, "Can you tell me where you were the night the ponies were taken?"

"I was at the stables. I left around 9:30 and went home and came back around 11:00 for a final check. Colonel, it's true we're hard pressed to take care of the medical expenses, but I'd never do anything wrong to get 'em paid."

"Because you were at the stables and no one else has been linked to the missing ponies and since you are a long-time associate with the college, I'll hold off on any formal action until further investigating has been completed. You may leave now; I'll be in touch with you later."

Jake left "Old Main" and walked dazed down to the stables. He was so distressed he was unable to properly collect his thoughts.

If only he could figure why anyone was out to get him. He thought, Whistlebottom took charge of the investigation as far as the campus people were concerned. He must have had Colonel Wyatt's ear. The police hadn't cast any guilt on him. They had questioned him and left it at that.

Kit rounded the corner of the stables and ran smack into Jake, surprising them both. "Sorry about that Jake. You allright?"

"I'm okay physically, but I'm troubled over people trying to pin the blame on me."

"Who is?"

"I don't really know, but Colonel Whistlebottom seems to be the one who sparks all the questions. Colonel Wyatt questioned me, but I don't think he believes I'm guilty. He seems like he is checking me out because some one is implicating me to him. Colonel Whistlebottom came to me and told me to report to Colonel Wyatt. I've never done anything to him, I don't know why he'd be after me."

"I believe in you, Jake. I'll keep my eyes open."

Meanwhile, Whistlebottom decided to ease off from the Gretel affair. Although not happy about it, she agreed because of Agnes' suspicions.

Before Gretel linked herself to Winston, she had extended certain liberties to a cadet in return for favors. She continued the relationship occasionally while she carried on with the Colonel. And she managed a complicated balancing act. Now she would revert to her original arrangement and quit being a paramour.

Chapter XXVI

Kit had a weekend furlough at home. He explained to Mary Lou that he had an affair of some urgency in Chester.

He changed to his civilian clothes, took his mother's car and left for Chester to find Big Cracker. Cruising all the streets in Frog Pond, he came up empty. He drove down Walnut Street bordering the college, turned on Seventeenth Street and went back down Providence Avenue. Turning back into Frog Pond, he drove to Gold Street and saw Big Cracker half-way down the street.

He braked to a sudden stop, jumped out of the car and ran up and pushed Cracker, who reeled back unexpectedly. Kit was all over him. Landing a looping right to the left eye, he made Cracker see shooting stars. He drew back his right and shot a crusher, squashing Cracker's nose, giving him the double feature of star gazing. Cracker said, "You son-of-bitch, I'll kill you." He reached for Kit hoping to get a headlock, throw him to the ground, and get his dirty Cracker tactics going. As he reached, Kit grabbed his wrist and twisted his arm up behind his back fast and hard causing a wretched pain in his shoulder socket. Kit yelled at him, "Who was your accomplice in the pony theft? I'll break your arm if you don't tell me." He added more pressure to the arm, producing a loud yelp from the big oaf. He half grunted and half mumbled "Gretel." Kit couldn't understand, he said, "Who?"

Cracker said more clearly, "Gretel."

Kit asked, "Was Jake involved?"

"Hell no" Cracker grunted, "He'd never do nothin' to them ponies. I don't know who helped her."

Kit gave another twist, "Why was Gretel mixed up in this?" Cracker told him she was a gambler and had run up a big debt she was having trouble paying. She agreed to help with the ponies so WMA would lose the match and the gamblers could win big, canceling her debt. The plan backfired, WMA won and she's still in debt. The gamblers would kill him for squealing. He'd need protection.

Kit told him he couldn't protect him, but he'd tell the police he cooperated. His mission completed, he released his arm.

Cracker said, "My arm feels broke." Then he mumbled, "You'll get yours when my gang catches you."

Kit stared, "You want more? I'm just warmed up. If I hear any more threats, you better hope I don't find you alone in one of these alleys."

Kit left Cracker with his nose bleeding, his eye puffing, holding his arm. Kit wondered who released the ponies for Gretel.

Chapter XXVII

Kit reported back to school on Monday and requested an appointment with the president. He told the secretary it was urgent. With very little delay, he was given his audience.

"Good morning, Fox. What's so urgent on this Monday morning?"

"Sir, I've had a verbal confession from one of the horsenappers. Two brothers from Frog Pond known as Big and Little Cracker represented a syndicate in a gambling plot." He related the story in full detail. When he got to the meaty part, he said, "And Gretel was the pivotal inside person in the plot. Perhaps she will name her accomplice, the one who released the ponies. Big Cracker said it wasn't Jake."

With a baffled expression, the Colonel said, "I never in my wildest dreams suspected Gretel. I'll question her before the police get here. We must locate the ponies. Who knows their condition?" The Colonel dismissed Fox with thanks.

Gretel could not be located; she was not in her apartment. Actually, she had been troubled, worried sick that she had gotten herself into such a fatuous situation. The gambling had done her in. She had gone to a movie down at the State Theater on 7th Street. She would be alone, undisturbed, able to think. If she turned herself in and cooperated before someone else came forth, she might be able to cop a deal. When Whistlebottom mentioned that the Crackers were involved, she knew the police would learn about her through them. Perhaps she'd be better off if she took off and hid out. If she confessed, she'd involve several people; she'd rather not. She came out of the movie, got her car and headed toward Wilmington instead of WMA.

The police, advised of Gretel's involvement, were on the lookout and spotted her car while she was in the movie theater. As she drove off, the police followed her and stopped her after she had driven three blocks. They took her to the police station for questioning, and during the interrogation, she confessed to her involvement, implicating the Cracker brothers. Asked of her whereabouts that night, she said she had been visiting a friend, and had gotten someone else to release the ponies.

Police Sergeant Laws said she must prove where she was and identify whoever it was that released the ponies or be charged with releasing them. Gretel needed time to think. If she disclosed her relationship with Whistlebottom, she'd admit being a paramour to all the college, while opening a can of worms for Agnes to deal with. That would cause a rumpus on campus. If she revealed who opened the gate, it could mean expulsion for the cadet. Opting not to involve the others, she was led to a cell for incarceration.

After a night in jail, she decided to reveal the cadet.

Colonel Wyatt advised Jake he was off the hook. As he and Kit celebrated his exoneration, Kit told him he never believed his guilt, but he never considered Gretel as the culprit. Also, her involvement with the Crackers and gambling was still an unexpected puzzle.

Colonel Wyatt had Whistlebottom in his office seated nervously across the desk from him. "Colonel, why were you pushing so hard to involve Jake? He was probably the most unlikely person on campus."

"There was really no other suspect until the Crackers implicated Gretel. She was also an unlikely suspect. I apologize for my accusation. I'll mention it to Jake." Whistlebottom wanted out from under.

"Are you sure you didn't have a reason for trying to implicate Jake? I expect a truthful answer."

"Colonel, I felt we should've resolved the theft as soon as possible. Jake was the logical choice. I frankly acted impulsively, I'm sorry."

"Whistlebottom, Jake's been hurt badly. You'd best make it up to him on the double," Wyatt's tone had Whistlebottom on his way to the stables.

Jake and Kit were still chatting when the Colonel approached. After asking to see Jake alone, the Colonel said, "I'm sorry, Jake, I acted too quickly. I misjudged you."

Jake looked at him; the Colonel couldn't hold the stare. He looked away. "I've never felt this way before, but I can' t accept the apology. It seems something's not out in the open. I thought I saw Gretel leaving your house the night of the theft. I stumbled as I left the house and it took me a few moments to regain my senses. When I did get up and walk away, I heard the rear door close and I saw her walk away from your house."

"You're mistaken, Jake. Gretel wasn't there. Did you ever mention it to anyone, what you thought you saw?" Whistlebottom was sweating.

"Of course not, it was none of my business. But since she's involved in the theft and you tried in every way to implicate me, it might be my business. One thing's sure, she couldn't have opened the gates to let the ponies out if she was with you. Excuse me, Sir."

Gretel told her plan of the theft at her arraignment. She talked one of the cadets into letting the ponies out who was willing to help because of the favors she granted him. She hand picked him because he knew the ponies, and they would follow him quietly. The cadet was Joe McKee.

The campus was shocked. Joe was the last one on the polo team anyone would have suspected. He was quiet, rather shy and perceived as a role model.

Kit never considered Joe; he was so straight. He thought it might have been Al Tyler, but not Joe. Kit went to Joe's room. Released to the custody of the college officials, Joe sat staring out the window as Kit arrived. "Joe, what happened? Is Gretel telling the truth?"

"I'm afraid she is. She encouraged a relationship between us. I didn't realize how she wanted to use me. I was flattered by the sexual favors she offered. She asked me to let the ponies out onto the practice field - simply as a prank - give Jake something to worry about. I just led them onto the field and left. I didn't know they were to be taken away. I was foolish. I had never had a relationship like the one with Gretel. Actually, I probably would have done most anything, rather than end the affair."

Kit smiled, "It may not be as bad as I thought, you are guilty of a prank and a stupid one at that, but you didn't know of the ultimate plan. If you explain it to Colonel Wyatt, he may consider the circumstances."

"I have an appointment with him in an hour. I'll find out then," Joe said, with a look of concern.

Chapter XXVI11

Jake sat in the President's office fidgeting with his riding crop. "Colonel, I didn't think to report this before, but since Gretel is involved in the theft, I feel I should. When I went to Colonel Whistlebottom's home to report the ponies missing, I saw Gretel leave by the back door. But the Colonel denies she was there. It may mean nothing, but why would he keep trying to pin it on me?"

"Jake, it doesn't mean he is involved, but it does raise some questions I should ask. Thanks for bringing it to me." The Colonel stood as Jake got up to leave.

Colonel Wyatt was working on some financial details when Cadet McKee arrived. He returned his salute, put him at ease and told him to have a seat. "Mr. McKee, you know why you're here. What I want is your version of your involvement in the now famous 'Pony Theft.'"

"Sir, it is true, I was involved with Gretel. She swept me off my feet. She sort of singled me out, charmed me and I fell for her. I never had a relationship to equal it. It was all new to me, if you know what I mean. She suggested I let the ponies out as a lark on Jake. I know it wasn't a nice thing to do, Jake is such a fine, loyal person. I had no idea of the 'Pony Theft.' As soon as I let them out, I left the area. I didn't know they were taken away. Unfortunately, I was so taken with Gretel, I'd have done most anything she asked. I apologize for my stupid actions. I will make an apology to the Corps if you think it appropriate."

"It's been decided that no formal charges will be made against you. You were unaware of the plot. However, you're to be reprimanded for actions unbecoming to a Cadet. As of now, you are no longer a member of the polo team. You will be permitted to complete your studies and get your degree and commission. I'm disappointed in your behavior, but your exemplary character up to now kept me from an immediate dismissal. Now, get back to your duties," Wyatt nodded.

"Yes Sir. Thank you, Sir." He stood up, saluted and turned to leave the office.

Colonel Winston Whistlebottom was next. He stood at attention in front of Colonel Wyatt's desk, waiting for a return salute. It came with an, "At ease, Colonel."

"Colonel Whistlebottom, tell me about your relationship with Gretel. Jake saw her leaving your house the night of the 'Pony Theft.' Please don't spare the details. One thing seems certain. She was seeing Cadet McKee and you the commandant at the same time."

"Colonel, please understand, this is a very delicate subject, should Agnes find out, I'm not sure what would become of my marriage," he began to plead.

"You should have thought of that sooner."

"Yes, you're right. I've been having an affair with Gretel whenever my wife left to visit her mother which was about every six or seven months."

"I expect an honest answer. Were you involved in the 'Pony Theft'?"

"No, frankly, I knew nothing about it."

"Well, Colonel, I'm asking you for your voluntary resignation. If I don't get it, I'll be forced to terminate you. It would be much cleaner the former way. The reason being that you aren't the one we want commanding the Corps."

"Sir, you shall have it post haste," Whistlebottom rose, saluted and departed.

Eventually, he leveled with Agnes. Actually, she wasn't extraordinarily surprised, but she was humiliated. If he had been more discreet, perhaps the whole college would have been unaware. Now they would think she was unable to fulfil his needs. She hoped she would get the opportunity to return the favor.

The District Attorney's office prepared the case against Gretel and the Cracker brothers. Having confessed, Gretel was terminated from her position at the college for her affair with the cadet.

Chapter XXIX

With the "Pony Theft" under control and the ponies returned, the looming polo championship was the big attraction on campus. WMA and Yale were to clash in the Madison Square Garden event.

McKee's replacement seriously concerned Coach Fischer and the team. Replacing anyone on the starting four meant a step-down for one of the best polo teams in the country. The two players under consideration were Ryan, an experienced senior who was conservative but a great rider, and Joe Tersa an underclassman, lacking experience but a hard riding goal shooter, missing often but making some spectacular goals.

Ryan and Tersa had competed against each other the entire season. Coach Fischer decided to move Ryan up to the first unit because of his experience. During practice, Ryan fit in well, but naturally McKee's absence was a concern. Riding together so long, they played like a well-oiled machine, however, with a newcomer, the machine did not run as smoothly.

The Garden was a sellout. Since polo was popular in New York, the intercollegiate championship brought out all the faithful followers. The Corps paraded into the sports complex, accompanied by the marching band. Rousing applause greeted them as they moved to their seating section.

The first two chukkers featured a goal by a Yalie and a goal each by Beels and Kit, giving WMA a 2 to 1 lead. Yale tied the score at the start of the third chukker. Yale missed a goal, and Tyler shot, missing wide. Suddenly, a Yale rider broke out of the pack, striking the ball toward the goal. It looked like a sure score until Kit, aboard Win, got an angle on the Eli and rode him down. Stealing the ball, he hit it over to Tyler. Tyler did a spectacular job striking the ball down the field. Beels was open with a clear shot but Tyler elected to take a difficult shot, which came up short. Kit was following closely along with a Yalie who nudged him, keeping him from making the shot. Tersa, substituting for Ryan, came thundering up behind Kit and tapped the ball in for the goal that held up. WMA won the coveted indoor championship, 3 to 2.

Joe Tersa was the hero of the day. Everyone congratulated him. He was in a euphoric daze never dreaming of a celebrity status on a championship polo team. And at Madison Square Garden, the indoor sports mecca of the modern world!

The Cadet Corps was cheering wildly. As the players dismounted, the Corps and fans came onto the field, congratulating the players from both teams. Mary Lou, Gerry and Phil found Kit and the rest of the team surrounded by well wishers. They worked their way through the crowd to give him an emotional hug. Mary Lou favored him with a huge hug and a kiss. In spite of just finishing the polo match of his life, he felt the kiss through his entire body. "We have furlough tomorrow, I'd like to spend it with you."

Mary Lou's face brightened, "It seems like such a long time since we spent a day together; let's go on a picnic. I'll pack the lunch."

Kit answered, "That would be perfect, let's plan on it. The team has to go to center field for the trophy presentation. Then we must return to college. I'll see you tomorrow as soon as I arrive home."

The trophy was received by the entire team, the coach and Jake, who was along as the trainer. Each one received a gold medal imprinted with a polo player in action on the front and Indoor Intercollegiate Polo Champions 1934 inscribed on the rear. The exhilaration was so great, Kit and Tyler actually had a few civil words.

When Kit arrived home on Sunday, Mary Lou was waiting with lunch, soda pop and an apple pie. It was such a beautiful day they opted for horseback instead of the old truck Gerry kept for the stable chores.

They rode to the Tyler Arboretum trail enjoying the beautiful forests, steams and ponds. They found a tempting spot for a picnic: a clearing in a sylvan setting with a thick ground cover of moss. They dismounted, got the picnic basket and spread a thick blanket. So anxious to share their emotions, they embraced, kissed passionately and sank down on the blanket, the lunch forgotten.

While the love they made was inhibited by clothes, they shifted and squirmed eventually satisfying their inexperienced desires, hoping no one would wander down the trail.

Mary Lou said softly, "Oh, how I love you. Wouldn't it be wonderful if we could enjoy the luxury of a bed for our love making?"

"Yes, it would. Thinking of how you feel gives me a perfect opportunity. How about getting married after I graduate in June? If you say 'yes,' I'll ask your Dad."

They spread out the lunch enjoying the shelter of trees along with the chicken salad sandwiches garnished with pickles and olives. They finished up with the apple pie Kit kept eyeing during lunch. Mary Lou offered a piece of sharp mouse cheese to go with the pie saying, "Apple pie without the cheese is like a kiss without a squeeze."

With that, Kit took the cheese saying, "Perish the thought," and gave her a kiss with a hard squeeze. She loved it.

They picked up, both anxious to get back to Mary Lou's, so Kit could speak to Mr. Folkner. They mounted and rode off toward Lima.

Kit really hadn't planned what he'd say. He'd have his degree; he would work with Gerry; he'd stay in the army reserves. He felt he would be a good provider.

Mary Lou let him go in the house without her. He found Mr. Folkner in the kitchen making iced tea. Even though he knew the family so well, he felt nervous. He thought, "Damn the torpedoes," here goes nothing.

"Mr. Folkner, may I have a word with you?"

"Of course, Kit. Sit down. Have some iced tea."

"Thank you, Sir, just some sugar, please. Mary Lou and I...let me start again. Mary Lou agreed...let me put it this way. I would like to ask you for Mary Lou's hand in marriage. I love her with all my heart, I'll work hard to provide for her, I'll protect her. Will you consent, Sir?"

"Kit, our whole family knows and likes you already, like one of our own. As I think about it, yes, I'll consent but we would like Mary Lou to finish college and that means a two-year wait. You know as you two go through life, if anything happened to you, she would be better prepared to face the job market if she had a degree. Also, keep in mind the seriousness of marriage, my family and yours, too, view it as a permanent arrangement, not to be taken lightly."

"I'm well aware of everything you say, Sir. We both feel so much can happen in two years. Why not be able to start to enjoy each other now? She tells me Mrs. Folkner was only nineteen when you were married, and my mother was very young, too. Believe it or not, we know there are risks to marriage, but we are both ready to take them."

"Kit, you have our blessings, all we want for you both, is a life full of happiness."

"Thank you, Sir. If you don't mind, I want to go find Mary Lou and give her the good news."

"By all means."

Chapter XXX

While Kit and Mary Lou planned their wedding, the trial of Gretel and the Cracker brothers commenced.

The courthouse was in Media, the County seat, a quaint town with shops, restaurants and professional offices with residences surrounding the business district. A trolley and a local train served the public transportation needs.

The District Attorney's office built a case against all the defendants: Gretel and the Cracker brothers. With McKee and Whistlebottom as witnesses for the prosecution, they felt they had an airtight case.

Gretel was represented by a small town lawyer who was a clever negotiator by the name of Sebastian. The syndicate hired a top criminal barrister from Philadelphia to represent the Cracker brothers.

They were all charged with stealing the ponies. Gretel was also charged with aiding and abetting an illegal gambling venture, the Crackers with running the illegal gambling venture.

The case was heard before Judge Corbey in Court Room #1. The defendants, their attorneys, and District Attorney Ernest Preen were present when the Judge took the bench.

When Gretel was asked, she pleaded guilty, as advised by Sebastian considering the evidence and witnesses in this case. Sebastian negotiated with Ernie Preen regarding her options. The DA agreed to a suspended sentence with six months probation due to her previously unblemished record.

The Crackers, on the other hand, pled not guilty on the advice of their attorney, a Mr. Shadely. He planned to get them off by tampering with the witnesses.

Mr. Shadely received unequivocal instructions from the syndicate to keep them out of it, and to make it clear, if necessary, that the syndicate had no connection with the Crackers; they were acting on their own.

The witnesses Shadely was to approach were Whistlebottom and McKee. Whistlebottom received an anonymous call requesting a meeting. He met two men at a diner at 5:30 in the morning. They came right to the point. The older of the two said, "We don't want any testimony from you that would help to incriminate the Cracker brothers. If you don't agree, you and your family will be in serious jeopardy. Do I make myself clear?"

"I understand."

McKee was contacted similarly but arranging his meeting was more difficult because of his cadet restrictions. When they finally met, the same demands were made. McKee told them he understood.

The other witness offering Shadely concern was Gretel, she could give damaging testimony, but he felt he could handle her on the witness stand.

Shadely didn't count on what happened next.

Both McKee and Whistlebotttom reported the overtures they had received to their attorneys. The matters were brought before the court and after thorough investigation, Mr. Shadely was terminated as counsel for the Cracker brothers and subjected to judicial penalties. This turn of events implicated the syndicate, broadening the scope of the case.

Chapter XXXI

Agnes was peeling the potatoes in the kitchen of their new residence at Fort Dix. During her menial household chores, her mind wandered over the recent events affecting her life, particularly the philanderings of Winston. She was anxious to return the favor, as it were.

In the past, his lascivious activities were performed when she visited her mother. With this in mind, she determined those visits would become necessary if her plan was to work.

She would announce her plans to visit her mother well in advance and hopefully, Winston would plan his lustful escapades. The consequences of his involvement with that tramp Gretel made her doubtful, however, there was no need for her doubts.

Always on the prowl, Whistlebottom noticed a buxom cow working in the post exchange. She seemed receptive to his overtures, and that started his proverbial motor running.

Over dinner in their combination kitchen and dining area, Agnes said, "I'll be going to visit my mother in three weeks. She hasn't been feeling well."

"What's the trouble now?"

"She's had migraines on and off recently. She's been upset ever since your problem at WMA."

"Everything seems to revolve around that incident lately. I'd like to forget it." He shoved a large forkful of mashed potatoes in his mouth.

As she finished her last bite of chicken she said, "You should pray for forgiveness and maybe it will stop nagging at you."

"It's not nagging at me; it's just that it keeps popping up. You know she planned it all. I just happened to be at the wrong place at the wrong time."

"Oh, come now, Winston, the incident took place in our home. Don't insult my intelligence. The more you talk the more ridiculous you sound."

Winston pushed his chair back from the table saying, "My dear, let's just forget it and try to get on with our lives."

Whistlebottom, given yet another lease on his sexual prowess, decided to look for the buxom cow. His aide had learned her name. Eve. She was working as a civilian employee in charge of purchasing at the PX. He spotted her after wandering about for a few minutes. When she took a breather, he eased over next to her.

He said, "Excuse me, Eve, I know we've nodded before, but I've just learned your name. I'm Winston Whistlebottom. I wondered if you might have some free time when we might get better acquainted."

She thought to herself, a Colonel would be a welcomed change compared to that sloppy old Buck Sergeant I dumped last week. "I think we might arrange a meeting. Why don't you pick me up after work at 7:30?"

"I'll be there."

After dinner, Whistlebottom told his wife he had some details to attend to but he wouldn't be late.

Taking a circuitous route to the PX, he found Eve waiting by the door. As he pulled over to the curb, Eve walked over to the car hesitantly, looked in the window and recognized the Colonel. He reached across the front seat, opening the door for her. She jumped in.

"Well, hi! Where are you taking me?"

"Maybe just for a drive I have some time constraints that came up suddenly. They come along with the territory. I never know when; I'm on alert most of the time."

"Does that mean we can't make better plans if we pursue a relationship? It's not good enough. I expected to go somewhere, have dinner and dance."

Whistlebottom thought, I can't chance being seen with this cow near the base and I don't want to spend a long evening with her till I know what to expect. "If I know far enough in advance, I can do a better job arranging my schedule. For now, we'll take that ride and chat a little."

"Well, maybe tonight, but you'll have to do better the next time."

They drove around the base until Whistlebottom saw the spot he was looking for, secluded and deserted. He pulled into the area and switched off the lights. "It's easier to concentrate on you when I'm not driving." He leaned over and put his arms around her shoulders trying to pull her over to him. She slid over, reluctantly.

Eve thought, I'm not going to make this easy, he has yet to spend a cent on me and he's ready to make a pass. "Aren't you rushing it a bit?"

"No, not really. We don't have much time tonight. How can we tell if we're attracted to each other if we don't share some hugging and kissing?"

"O.K., but don't think I'm some first-time easy lay. Come to think of it, I've decided you'd appreciate it more if it took you some time and you had to work for it. Perhaps I'll become celibate."

"I don't believe you would waste all your attractive endowments." He looked directly in her eyes then kissed her. She returned the kiss with enthusiasm pushing her two melon-sized breasts into his chest. It was too much for him and he eased his hand onto her breast. She let it remain there for a few seconds so that he'd remember it, then she put her elbows to work moving it away. "Not so fast, Colonel. We're just getting acquainted, remember. Slip into neutral and relax."

"Okay, Okay. Just one more kiss, then I must take you home." They lingered over an emotional kiss with Eve eventually breaking it off.

The Colonel got home early as he had promised.

The time arrived for Agnes to leave for her mother's, and she left promptly as planned. She felt sure Winston had a red hot arrangement with some bimbo. She was hoping he did.

For sure, the Colonel had made his plans. He had agreed to take Eve out for dinner and dancing away from the base and then return to her apartment for a nightcap and who knew what. He hoped she hadn't become celibate.

He was to pick her up at her apartment. As he drove, he tried to figure a way they could just stay at her apartment, make an omelette and then..."Fat chance."

He spotted her at the door of her building. When she saw his car, she came over. He jumped out and opened her door. After he got in the car, she said immediately, "I'm starved. How about the Jersey Steak House?"

"That would be great." So much for the omelet.

They both ordered T-Bones, baked potatoes and salad. The food and service were good.

The Steak House featured a small ten-piece band with first and second trumpets, two saxes, a trombone, drums, a piano, a bass, a guitar and a clarinet. The Colonel and Eve danced cheek to cheek to their sweet, slow numbers with Eve humming badly off key. He wished she'd rub herself against him and quit the humming. She was sort of a clumsy dancer, not following well and stepping on his corn so hard he wanted to yell. When the fast numbers were played, he suggested they sit them out. But no, she wanted to jitterbug; he was already starting to limp. The clumsy cow didn't know the first thing about jitterbugging. She was never in step, bumping into the other couples, giving them a hard nudge with her big rump. Had he not anticipated the "big show" back at her apartment, he would have dumped her.

At 11:30, she agreed to leave.

It was a short ride to her apartment house. After they entered, she turned and kissed him.

He took off his coat and loosened his tie, taking her into his embrace, they exchanged heated kisses. She unbuttoned his shirt while he unzipped the rear zipper on her dress. He slipped the dress off her shoulders and it fell to the floor, revealing her full figure in bra and pants. He couldn't take his eyes off her huge breasts. They finished undressing working their way toward the bedroom.

The Colonel said, "I've waited for this moment anxiously."

As they lay down on the bed naked, she said, "Are you sure you're ready?" looking at his organ which had yet to respond.

"Kiss me and you'll get a big surprise."

They kissed and she rolled over with the "old boy" now on top in perfect position. They kissed some more, pumped back and forth, still nothing happened. He was starting to feel a little embarrassed. This had never happened before.

Eve said, "Well, Colonel, where is this big surprise you have for me? I'm waiting. Is it you who has become celibate? Are you going to perform or shall we call it an evening?"

Embarrassed and confused, he said, "I suppose we should call it an evening." He got dressed quickly then turned to her saying, "I'll be raring to go tomorrow; I'll give you a call."

As he opened the door to leave, she said, "Don't call me, I'll call you."

Driving home he thought to himself, it must have been that clumsy cow that turned me off.

About this time, Agnes was just climbing into bed at her parents' home. She wondered to herself, DID THE SALT PETER WORK WINSTON? She had laced his food with it for the last three weeks.

CHAPTER XXXII

With graduation approaching, Kit realized how quickly the last four years had passed. The wedding date was set for June, following shortly after graduation. Both his and Mary Lou's parents were very pleased with the impending union. He planned to work in the family business and keep his military career active by staying in the army reserves as a Second Lieutenant. Keeping the reserve status meant duty one weekend a month and two weeks in the summer. If a national emergency cropped up, the reservists were the first to be called.

The wedding was a magnificent affair, starting with the ceremony at St. Peter's Church in Chester with Pancho standing as best man and Hedy as maid of honor. The reception followed at the Folkner home where the weather cooperated with the outdoor festivities, and the partying went on well into the night.

The guest list was extensive and included among many others, the members of the polo team with the exception of Tyler. Kit was especially pleased to see Jake. He had been depressed by the accusations; he, who had never anything but wholesome, affectionate thoughts about WMA, the cadets and his beloved horses. To think that he would have considered an offensive act toward any of them almost gave him a mental breakdown. However, surviving the ordeal, he was at the reception in his Sunday finest. When he congratulated Kit, he looked him in the eyes, saying, "Thank you, son, for the support you gave me. I'll never forget it."

"Jake, I could never imagine you doing those things and I had confidence in your innocence. Mary Lou and I felt it wouldn't have been a complete reception without you. Thanks for being here to share our happy moments with us."

Pancho and Hedy were flirting recklessly in the receiving line. They laughed and looked longingly into each others eyes. Pancho had told Kit they had considered marriage, but Hedy wasn't sure she wanted to live in Cuba. Having never been there, she was unaware of the beauty of the island. Also, her parents were doing what they could to convince her not to go so far away. And Pancho was definitely going back to Cuba. Hedy's options were to go to Cuba or not get married. She elected to delay her decision, not wanting to disappoint her parents or break off her relationship with Pancho. She needed time to think it through. Pancho wasn't happy with her delay but went along with it, realizing once he returned to Cuba, their relationship might fizzle out with distance being what it was.

The newlyweds left on the ferry from Woods Hole for a ten-day honeymoon at Nantucket. They enjoyed the strolls on the beach. Catching blues deep-sea fishing, they cleaned and cooked them in their honeymoon cottage then enjoyed them by candlelight. They sailed to Martha's Vineyard, visiting the quaint shops and lunching on delicious lobster. Back on Nantucket, they made passionate love whenever it struck their fancy and found a love that could last forever. When the time came to depart, the beautiful little island had etched itself permanently into their fondest memories.

Chapter XXX111

Kit and Mary Lou found an attractive second floor apartment bordering the WMA campus. They enjoyed the short walk to downtown Chester. On Saturday nights they walked to the stately Stanley Theater to be entertained by a movie featuring Clark Gable or Dick Powell and a stage show with perhaps the famous big band of Woody Herman. Afterward, they stopped at Davis' Pharmacy for an ice cream soda.

The family business was changing from ice and coal to heating fuels, refrigerators, and oil heating systems. The ice business was fading with more families using the electric refrigerator. These changes prompted the development of a larger service department to maintain and repair the new oil heating systems.

Kit reported to the service department on his first day at work after the honeymoon. Teaming with Shorty Mitchell installing and maintaining heating systems, he embraced the job with enthusiasm and intelligence. They were the fastest team in the plant.

They were assigned an oil heating system installation in the remote rural community of Elwyn. The home was an enormous twelve roomer with a hot air gravity coal fired heating system. The relic was to be replaced with an oil fired system.

The house sat on a 150-acre site, and was owned by a horseman called Will Bell. He had an enviable stable of thoroughbreds among which were some fine race horses.

As Kit and Shorty drove up the long driveway, they spotted a big red stallion feeding in the pasture. The sound of the truck interrupted his grazing; he raised his huge muscular neck and looked directly at them, shook his head, then returned to his feed. Kit had seen this one-of-a-kind race horse before, but Shorty had not. There was not a more impressive horse on earth.

They pulled around to the rear of the house, emerged from the service truck and knocked on the door. A friendly butler greeted them saying they were expected. He led them down the basement stairs to the heating system. Since the heating needs were already surveyed, they were ready to install the new system.

After two days of intense work, the installation was nearing completion. Interested in seeing the remarkable system, Mr. Bell came down the cellar steps saying,"All right you young lads, how about showing me this new fangled heating system."

Kit looked up, recognizing him immediately. "Yes, Sir, Mr. Bell, it would be our pleasure. My partner here is Shorty Mitchell, and I'm Kit Fox. If you're ready, he'll explain it to you."

"Are you Gerry Fox's son?"

"Yes, Sir."

"I know your Dad. A fine man and a man of his word. What is he doing with that new mare he acquired down at Havre de Grace race track?"

Kit walked away from the heater, saying, "He hopes to race her for another year and then breed her. She's of good stock, named Misty."

"Well, give him my compliments and best wishes. Now let's see about this new heater."

Shorty explained in laymen's language the BTU'S, the grade of oil used, the maintenance requirements, the oil storage tank with its copper tube feeder to the heater. After many questions and answers, Mr. Bell was satisfied.

Bell looked at Kit, "Do you have the same love for horses your father has?"

"Yes, Sir, I was brought up on horses, I love 'em. I've been fortunate enough to do plenty of riding."

"If you two have a few extra minutes when you're finished, I'd like to introduce you to one of my best friends."

Kit and Shorty wrapped up the job and took their tools to the truck where Mr. Bell was waiting.

"Follow me!" He led them to a fenced pasture where the big horse waited for his owner. "Red was a triple crown winner. He has a stout heart and courage that never let him quit. He's a true champion."

Kit walked nearer, scrutinizing the big warrior, "I've seen him before when passing by but never at this close range. He's a legend. It might be presumptuous of me, Sir, but don't you think Red and Misty might produce a winner?"

"You do move quickly young man. Misty's not in Red's class. Maybe she'll prove something this season. You know, Red comes at a very heavy stud fee. It's not a likely prospect."

"Well, it didn't hurt to ask. It's a great treat to meet Red. Hope to see more of him."

Bell turned to Shorty, "Well, young man, what do you think of Red? You're not going to vie for his stud services, are you?"

"No, I'm not. I'm awed at his magnificence." Red trotted away. "What grace he has."

Mr. Bell walked them to the truck, they said their good byes and the truck rolled down the driveway.

Back at the business compound, Kit went to Gerry's office. Veronica, still the boss's secretary, told him his Dad was not with anyone and sent him in.

Gerry greeted Kit with his normal embrace saying, "It's good to see you. How did the Bell job go?"

Kit looked at his Dad, "It went fine; we just finished. Dad, he took us over to see Red. I asked him if Red might service Misty. He didn't encourage me, but he didn't say absolutely 'no.' Do you know him well enough to impose on him. I know their colt would be special. Misty is a smart, fast mare, and she should have a great season. Her training times have been spectacular in the mile. She'll get a lot of attention when she enters the field."

"You're right, Kit. She's a good one, and we'll have an interesting time when she's in competition. As far as Will Bell goes, I think your proposition is unlikely, but I'll think about it. You don't know it, but he loves the game of chance. Maybe that deserves some thought."

As Misty worked out, Gerry was getting reports from his trainer for 6 furlong times of 1:10 and 1:12 minutes. She ran a mile in 1:37.

Judge Hanna lived in Wawa, a stone's throw from Lima. His love for fox hunting was second only to his family, and when he entertained his friends, counted among them were many horse people.

Wawa, the Native American term for Wild Goose, was a small hamlet of attractive estates and the buildings of the Wawa Dairy Farm. The famed highway, Baltimore Pike, ran directly down the middle of the village. The countryside was beautiful rolling hills wooded with stately oaks and beeches.

The Hanna estate was a neat ten acre layout with a large stone Pennsylvania farmhouse, stable, pool and tennis court. The estate was ideal for entertaining, one of Mrs. Hanna's favorite pastimes.

Bunny Hanna's picnic list included both Gerry and Phil and Will and Beth Bell. The guests were told there would be swimming or tennis available. The horse people visited the Judge's stable to see the beautiful thoroughbreds.

At the bar by the swimming pool, Gerry and Will refilled their drinks after returning from the stable.

"My son was impressed with that big stud of yours. Thinks he and our new mare, Misty, would produce a winner. My thinking is Misty's right particular, Red may not even turn her head."

Knowing that Red is the most sought after stud, Will doesn't take the bait. "Your Misty has a long way to go before she'll entertain the likes of Red."

Gerry wasn't dismayed, he appealed to Will's penchant toward the game of chance. "Tell me neighbor, would you be willing to bet a Red stud service, with pay, that Misty won't win the Aberdeen Stakes this year? The race is about four months down the road; the field is exciting, maybe just a cut below the triple crown events."

"Now there's a gentleman's wager," Will answered as he took a sip, "I can't pass that one up. Your Misty is outclassed in that field. She won't be first across the line." He put out his hand to secure the wager.

Gerry shook his hand hoping Misty would run the race of her career.

Will felt so confident he told the Judge about it and asked if he wanted to make a small wager on Misty. The Judge declined saying, "She'll have her work cut out for her with that field. Thanks, but I'll pass that one."

Chapter XXXIV

In Misty's first race under Gerry and Kit, she drew the fourth post position. Of the ten horses in the field, none had won more than one race this season.

They all broke clean, on the first turn each fell into position. Misty was back in the pack running fifth comfortably. Coming out of the back stretch, Emanuel Gonzales gave her her head and pulled her to the outside. She passed the fourth horse coming out of the final turn chasing the third. Suddenly, she put on a burst of speed and passed the number three horse; she was gaining on the win and place positions as they crossed the finish line.

Gerry congratulated Manny but then asked him why he hadn't let Misty go sooner. Manny told him he didn't realize she had that kind of stamina. Manny rubbed Misty's nose and followed with, "She's got a great heart."

Kit offered, "She ran 1:12 for this six-furlong race, but will she have enough left when it comes to the Aberdeen Stakes Mile?"

"My plan," Gerry answered, "is to move her up to seven furlongs and then the mile. We'll work her up gradually. She had some respectable times in the mile last year. It is my hope that she'll peak just in time for the Aberdeen."

Misty's next race was another six-furlong: three-year olds and up. It wasn't the feature but she won it coming from the eighth position with a time of 1:12. Again Manny was up and rode a smart race; giving her her head earlier, she ran with encouraging speed.

The week after her last race, she developed a lung infection and the fever that went with it. The vet was called in and advised Gerry that she would be out of commission until the infection was cured. With the proper medication and rest, her recovery would take about ten days. Unfortunately, the illness lingered for twenty days, compounding the preparation for Aberdeen.

When the fever subsided, she was taken out for easy exercising. Her healing process was slow, but she was able to increase her training activities; in a week's time, she was able to run five furlongs. The next week she ran six, but her time was a slow 1:15 minutes. For some reason her trainer felt her heart was lacking the courage which had made her special.

The following week she resumed her competition running last in a six-furlong race. Manny reported she lacked the finishing kick she had before the illness.

Visiting her in the stable, Kit talked gently to her as he brushed her down. Misty seemed to enjoy these visits, her head coming up and ears perking when she heard Kit's voice as he was approaching. She was more frisky when Kit was about, but her illness took a lot out of her. She had a long way to go.

Her next race was a five-furlong. Breaking well from the fifth gate position, she moved down the back stretch running in second place. As they came around the final turn, Misty faded back into fourth place. Her stamina spent, she finished next to last at 1:03.

Manny reported, " She had nothing left; she faded. I never had to give her the whip before; she did it herself. I gave her some whip today, but she didn't or couldn't respond. Maybe you should rest her again. Let her regain her full strength."

Gerry responded, "I'm afraid I've pushed her getting ready for the Aberdeen. I thought she would be back by now. Let's give her ten days off then see how she is."

Kit agreed with his dad, hoping Misty would fully recuperate. When he asked Gerry for a few days off to give her his personal attention, Gerry agreed.

Kit spent his time at the stable working her out gingerly, careful not to tire her unduly. He brushed her down and generally nursed her, hoping to bring her back to her old self.

After the ten days of recuperation, they started serious workouts again. Her five, six and seven furlongs were disappointing, still lacking the spirited energy of her better days.

Gerry and Kit were on the verge of pulling her from the Aberdeen. The vet indicated the infection had not recurred, but she'd been weakened by it. Suddenly, Misty showed some signs of improvement. Her times were better in her workouts.

With only a month before the big race, Misty was put back into competitive racing. In two seven furlongs, she finished 5th and 6th. In her next race, the mile, she finished 4th. She lacked her great finishing drive. Her final tune up before Aberdeen was in a very good competitive mile. She was positioned in 3rd place on the back stretch, ideal to make her charge. She moved up to 2nd place rounding the final turn. Suddenly, she eased off the pace and fell back finishing 4th.

Manny, Kit and Gerry all realized she was well but worried why she had lost her final kick. With only a week, Kit decided to spend his free time boosting her fallen spirit. After her workouts, he talked to her, brushed and patted her. Once again, her ears perked up and she looked around at the sound of Kit's voice.

At breakfast, the day of the Aberdeen Stakes, Gerry voiced his concern, "Rascal with Jamie Esposito up has the fifth post position next to Misty. Jamie has always been an adversary of Manny's. He'll stop at nothing if he's in contention."

Kit looked at his Dad, "We can only hope Manny can steer clear of him."

"Finish up your breakfast so we can head down to the track."

They found Manny after he had ridden the third race and booted his horse in second. He asked them about Misty.

Gerry answered, "I just hope she feels as good as she looks."

"If her heart's in it, she'll give us a good race." Manny added.

"Jamie Esposito really concerns the hell out of me. All jockeys give you a bump if they can get away with it, but that Jamie is reckless. He'd bump hard enough to throw you off pace. I don't have to tell you to watch him. You've ridden against him many times. It's known no love's lost between you two."

"Gerry, I'll watch him, but I'll need eyes in the back of my head."

Kit went in to spend a few minutes with Misty before moving her to the paddock.

Her ears perked up when Kit spoke her name. She turned toward him, batting her eyelashes. He gave her an affectionate pat on her head, then her neck and shoulder. Speaking gently, he told her how much she meant to them all, what joy she brought to them, and to do the best she was able. He finished by telling her she was by far the best in the race. Kit thought she never understood a word, but when he gave her the final gentle slap, she nuzzled up to his shoulder, giving an affectionate snort. Kit wondered if maybe she'd gotten the message.

As Misty was announced, Gerry and Kit saw her come onto the track with Manny astride. There were eleven three-year olds in this famous stake race and all were starting their final warm up. As far as Gerry, Kit, Phil and Mary Lou were concerned, Misty was better looking than the rest of these beautiful bangtails, and she looked sharper and more confident. Truthfully, they only had eyes for her.

Misty was assigned gate Five, Rascal and Esposito were next door in gate Six. Misty approached and entered her gate without a hitch. Rascal was another matter. He was pushed, shoved and cajoled before he stubbornly went into the gate. Esposito sneered at Manny, "You don't think you'll win on that nag. Watch your arse - I'll be after it."

After the last five horses entered the gate, the bell rang and they were off. Misty went off at 20 to 1.

Down the back stretch, Rascal was running fourth and Misty fifth. In the final turn, Manny gave Misty her head, she edged to the outside. Misty moved nicely coming out of the final turn. Rascal had moved up to third, and Misty moved to fourth. As she pulled up even with Rascal, Esposito maneuvered Rascal to give them a bump, throwing Misty off stride. Rascal moved up taking over first place. Suddenly, Misty recovered showing her true grit. She ran past the third horse, then overtook the second while gaining on Rascal. It was now a two-horse race. At the finish line Misty gave her all. Rascal won by a nose.

There was silent disappointment in Gerry's box. Mary Lou suddenly shouted, "Look at the tote board." There in large letters was the word OBJECTION. Everyone waited tensely for the next two minutes. Then #6 horse DISQUALIFIED. The order of finish appeared. 5 Win, 2 Place, 7 Show. The disappointment turned into jubilation for the quartet in the box. They all went down to the winner's circle greeting Manny and Misty. Manny knew they wondered what had happened. He looked at Kit then Gerry, saying, "Esposito rode Rascal purposely into us, throwing us off the pace, costing us the race until the disqualification."

Will Bell came down, congratulating them on the win.

Gerry said, "Well, thanks, Will. I'm looking forward to that stud service of Red."

Will looked at him smiling. "You've got it."

Chapter XXXV

Kit was facing his two-week Army Reserve commitment. His communique from the U.S. Army directed him to report to the reserve armory in Chester. Rumor had it they would be on maneuvers at Camp Lee in Virginia.

To his surprise, when he arrived at the armory, he was told to report to Captain Dignazi's office. When Kit entered the office, Dignazi stood up and returned his salute. Smiling, he said, "Fox, you won't be going to Camp Lee. You've received orders to Lake Tahoe for a special assignment." He handed the orders to Kit. "They say you will be assigned to a proving grounds site where various recently developed munitions products would be tested."

"Sir, I requested duty in ordnance because of my interest in munitions. I'm very pleased to have orders to the proving grounds. What duty did you draw?"

Dignazi, yet another WMA alumnus said, "I'm a tank commander and I'll be going to Camp Jackson for a memorable two weeks -hot, humid, mosquitoes and snakes. I'm going to apply for flight training if I can get a regular army status. In the meantime, I'll settle for tank duty. Good luck at Tahoe."

With only two days before leaving his beloved Mary Lou, Kit intended to make the most of them.

They dined at the Naaman's Tea Room, a delightful little restaurant just over the state line in Claymont. A tender T-Bone steak, with baked stuffed potatoes and succotash was preceded by a hot cup of turkey soup with rice. All followed by a delicious dessert of apple pie a la mode.

When Mary Lou asked, Kit explained it'd take four days or so to Tahoe. He looked around the table candle and said, "I'll miss you, darlin'. I love you so much. While it's not a long time, it's the first time for us to be away from one another."

"I don't want you looking at any other girls out at that big lake," Mary Lou laughed.

"You know I've never had eyes for anyone but you. Now, I suggest we jump in our car and head for home. I'm going to make passionate love to you all night long."

"I thought you would never mention it. I'm anxious to be on our way."

On Sunday morning they attended the 8 o'clock services at the historic old St. Peter's Church on Broad Street. The early service gave them the rest of the day together. Bishop Tobin conducted the Communion Service with cut up cubes of bread and sherry wine. Those in attendance knelt at stations in front of the altar with their hands out to receive first the bread, then in a few moments the chalice with the wine. You were permitted to assist by tilting the eucharistic cup. If you dared to give it an enthusiastic tilt, you got an ounce and a half instead of a sip. Kit tried every time he took Holy Communion.

The minister customarily finished off whatever wine was remaining after all were served. After Bishop Tobin finished the remaining wine and terminated the service, he would appear a bit wobbly as he descended the four steps from the altar, particularly when he overestimated the members of the congregation taking communion. In this event, he would get three or four ounces to consume. What people didn't know was, the wine never bothered him. He always came down the steps backwards which was awkward and made him look wobbly.

As they left the church, the Bishop was at the door bidding each parishioner a good day. Mary Lou commented as they walked away from the church, "The Bishop seemed to stumble coming down the steps. His home is just across Broad Street from the church. Why don't we help him? He'll be going home after the 8 o'clock service."

Bishop Tobin was the Bishop of the Diocese of Pennsylvania. A priest at St. Peter's before he became the bishop, Bishop Tobin lived close to church remaining active but limiting his duties to the 8 o'clock Sunday morning service. In his early 70's, he was less physical in his later years.

Knowing the Fox family well, he followed Kit's career at WMA with special interest as he not only knew the family but his interest in WMA was also keen. When he had been the priest at St. Peter's he was also the chaplain at the college, serving the religious needs of the Corps.

When Kit and Mary Lou offered to escort him across the street, he made a feeble effort at rejecting their offer, "I'm perfectly able to get myself home. You young folks run along."

Kit followed with, "It's not that we really thought you needed the help; we thought it a good opportunity to exchange a few pleasantries."

"If you'll share a cup of tea or coffee and a sweet bun, I'll accept your offer."

Kit and Mary Lou agreed, and the three of them crossed Broad Street.

Seated comfortably at the dining room table, Bishop Tobin began telling them an interesting story.

"When I was a student at Drexel Institute in Philadelphia, I was invited to the home of a fellow student for a weekend. On Sunday afternoon before we left for school, his mother asked us to join her in the living room. She told me she had been working on my horoscope and she had finally finished it. She wanted to give me the results of her study. I urged her to continue. The thrust of the study was, I would seek another direction in my career after I graduated from college. I would deliberate; a forceful spiritual input would influence my choice. Eventually, I would rise to the top of my career choice. At that time, I had no idea that I would enter the ministry. I had planned a career in engineering.

"After I graduated from college, my mother grew, what we were told, terminally ill. My family pondered what to do short of prayer and a constant vigil. I went to church and prayed to God. I made a promise: if my mother's life was spared, I would devote my life to God. The next day she started feeling better, her fever subsided and the congestion in her lungs started to clear. She completely recuperated. The next semester, I enrolled in Divinity School.

"Little did my friend's mother know how accurate her prediction was."

Kit and Mary Lou loved the story. Kit said, "Have you ever looked back on what might have been?"

"Of course. But I've never regretted my decision. My life has been completely fulfilled by my calling to the ministry."

"My Dad has known you forever, but he never told me that story," Kit said, as he finished his cup of tea.

"Kit, I'm not sure I ever told him. He may like to hear it from you. Be my guest."

Mary Lou finally got up, "Bishop Tobin, thank you for the wonderful visit. Kit and I have a few stops to make before we go home and pack for Kit's duty at Lake Tahoe."

"Well, Kit, have a great experience and hurry home. We'll all miss you. Especially Mary Lou."

Mary Lou and Kit left the Bishop and took care of their other obligations.

Their last stop was a roast beef Sunday night dinner with Gerry and Phil and Mr. and Mrs. Folkner.

CHAPTER XXXVI

Kit boarded the train in Philadelphia for the first leg of his trip to Chicago. The Chicago Limited was one of those magnificent trains of the Thirties: beautiful dining car with silver place settings, crystal and linen; luxurious club car and most accommodating Pullman and coach cars.

With Pullman accommodations, he quickly found his compartment and settled in. Kit was in the dining car, enjoying a delicious cup of shrimp bisque, a light salad and two tender lamb chops, supplied by the famous Philadelphia Margarim Meat Company, when he surprisingly saw the famed "Horse Shoe Curve."

Since train travel was rather boring, the passengers enjoyed whatever attractive views there were. To pass the time, Kit made an occasional trip to the club car, striking up conversations with new acquaintances. What time he spent in his compartment was consumed by stretching out with a new novel called "Gone With The Wind."

The first leg of his trip ended as he pulled into Chicago, the busiest railroad station in the world, where Kit was required to change over to the Santa Fe line for his trip on to San Francisco.

Several hours into the trip, while reading the Chicago Tribune, he glanced up thinking he saw a familiar face. Short of staring, he looked more closely. It was no one he could place, but the face reminded him of someone. He went back to his newspaper, but the face lingered in the depths of his mind.

Spending the rest of the day sightseeing, chatting with new acquaintances and reading, Kit retired at 11:30. As he closed his eyes, the face came back to him. He suddenly was able to place it. It was Mr. Shadely, the Cracker brothers' unscrupulous attorney.

Morning found Kit leaving his compartment for breakfast when he came face to face with Mr. Shadely. Kit recovered quickly, excused himself, then asked, "Are you Mr. Shadely , sir?"

"I am young man, and who might you be?"

"I'm Kit Fox. I followed the Cracker brothers' case closely. I was a cadet at WMA at the time and a friend of McKee's. I knew Gretel, the dietitian and Colonel Whistlebottom, the commandant. Whatever happened to you?"

Shadely answered, "Normally, I'd ignore that question, but it's public record. I made a full confession and received an eighteen-month prison term. While I was in prison, I got religion and was ultimately released at the end of twelve months on good behavior. I have been disbarred and am going to California to look for a new start."

Kit questioned, "Why has the trial not started again?"

"My former colleagues advised me that the trial was about to commence as I was released from prison.

"The syndicate was unhappy with its implication when I was found out trying to witness tamper. I'm concerned the powers that be may seek retribution. Seldom is a situation like I created left dangling. I hope somehow I can get lost in L.A."

Kit looked at Shadely, "What about your family?"

"I'm divorced, no problem there."

"Well, Mr. Shadely, I hope things work out for you. I won't detain you any longer."

At breakfast Kit was joined by a distinguished looking gentleman who politely introduced himself as Mr. Robert Reson. After some preliminary conversation, Kit learned that Reson was a railroad agent allegedly traveling to San Francisco to pick up the trail of some criminals who'd been robbing passengers aboard west coast trains. The conversation flowed from one subject to another and eventually led to where they were from. Kit was dumbfounded when Reson told him he was from Chester. Kit told him of his own Chester ties, his present reserve officer status and recent graduation from WMA.

Reson commented, "I know of a Gerry Fox. Quite a well-known business man. I don't suppose you're related?"

"He just happens to be my dad. I work for him. Do you know the Ginettis? They're my mother's family."

"Sure do. They ran the great grocery store. Did you know the Cuthrys? They were my wife Gloria's family."

"I can't say that I did, but I'm sure my folks knew them."

"Are you on official duty now?", Kit asked as he took a bite of toast.

"No. But when I ride a train to my next assignment, I'm constantly to be aware and on the lookout for anything of an unusual or suspicious nature. Come to think of it, have you met Mr. Shadely in your travels?"

Kit looked at him, "Why, yes, I've met him. Why do you ask?"

"I had a chat with him and he seemed to be a nervous itch...like something was bothering him."

"It's funny you'd notice. He's actually concerned that he's been targeted by the syndicate."

"Why are they after him?"

"It's a long story so I'll give you the short version." When he finished, Reson showed his usual interest in the tale.

Jackie "The Cobra" Cousin had boarded the train in Chicago. His orders were to terminate that lawyer called Shadely, the fool that drew the syndicate into the law's clutches by witness tampering. Prior to that incident, the syndicate had been a silent partner, unobserved.

The Cobra, like his namesake, was famous for his quick strike. He took his victims out so fast they seldom saw it coming. He also had a fetish for careful planning...the reason he was a survivor.

The Cobra observed his victims, studying their moves and routines, i.e. mealtimes, cocktail times, bedtimes. Did they obviously carry a weapon? His plan was to get Shadely alone and stab him to death...a quiet mission drawing no one's attention to it. He would make his move just as the train was making a stop, accommodating his get away.

The next scheduled stop was Topeka, some hundred and fifty miles down the track, the spot where The Cobra was planning on making his move. More importantly, the opportunity had to present itself at the right time.

Concerned about Shadely's worried demeanor, Reson decided to keep him under observation. Not being on assignment, he thought it a good way to practice his skills. The trick, of course, was to tail him without being obvious. Shadely was easy to observe, wanting to be around people rather than be alone worrying about his plight. He spent much of his time visiting in the club car.

Shadely spotted Kit relaxing in the club car. He went over to greet him and chat a bit.

"Mr. Fox, do you mind if I join you for a few moments?"

"No, not at all."

"I have a strange feeling about my security. I've seen no one to cause me concern. It's a clairvoyant feeling."

Kit looked at him, "Those feelings are often meaningful. I wouldn't take it lightly. Be careful, don't be alone more than you have to be. Keep your eyes peeled for anyone who looks suspicious."

"The only person I've seen looking at me is an attractive middle-aged lady. She appears at the dining car when I'm there and usually at the club car when I visit it. I haven't thought of her in a suspicious way. It seemed to me her appearance was purely coincidental."

"Did you ever think maybe she has an interest in you? Why don't you go speak to her the next time you see her looking at you?"

Cobra was a well-dressed, inconspicuous, deceptive hit man. He was medium height and build, soft spoken, with a ruthless streak. Most of those who knew him thought he was possessed by an evil demon. Traveling with him was his attractive girl friend. He was able to trust her completely, so he thought. She proved from time to time to be useful to him, helping to carry out his schemes. She preferred to be called Honey Bea.

Seated in his compartment, he briefed her on his plan. She was to invite Shadely to the compartment under the guise of offering sexual favors. Once they were in the compartment, Cobra would make an appearance at which time she was to leave quickly. Cobra would then make his move.

Honey Bea Chase had been born and raised in Chicago, the daughter of a traveling preacher. Her mother was a seamstress who worked at home, caring for her daughter while Preacher Chase was on the road.

In her sixteenth year, Honey Bea quit school to marry an automobile mechanic. The first six months were filled with excitement and bliss. In the eighth month of their marriage, Gene lost his job. As they had trouble making ends meet, Gene became short fused. Unable to get a permanent job, he took to drink and was abusive. He drifted from one job to another and drinking most of what little money he made. The marriage lasted two years; Honey Bea took back her maiden name.

Needing an assistant, Preacher Chase asked Honey Bea to join him on the road and she agreed to give it a try. For the next fifteen years they worked together. Honey Bea eventually tried her own hand at preaching. Her sermons were well received as not only was she an attractive young dazzler, but she had an interesting delivery, talking about the sacrifice of Jesus Christ for the salvation of mankind and how it affected her: leading her to a life of preaching the work of God thus fulfilling her life.

Preacher Chase worked hard but barely eked out a living. His congregations were usually sparse and poor as were the collections. In his old pick up, he traveled the remote countryside. The bed of his truck was packed with his church tent, portable cooking stove, folding chairs and an altar. In good weather, he climbed up on the bed of the truck and preached his sermon. He took to his tent in the inclement weather.

Honey Bea, with her intriguing name and sensuous looks blending with interesting sermons, was developing a following. Many were young men.

The young men began waiting around after the service under the pretense of receiving divine guidance, while actually hoping to meet with Honey Bea. Being blessed with sensitive sexual desire, she welcomed these rendezvous.

The circuit Chase travelled started in Illinois then through Iowa, Nebraska, Kansas and Missouri. After Honey Bea started preaching at the second circuit turn, the congregations grew and more money contributions were developed. Preacher Chase's sermons improved, inspired by Honey Bea's success. They found people waiting when they arrived in town.

Preacher Chase was aware of the rendezvous taking place, but he was unaware of the other developments.

Honey Bea offered these young men additional spiritual opportunities. For a stipend they could partake in what she called "Heaven on Earth." When the Preacher had retired, "Heaven on Earth" took place in the bed of his truck. Word of mouth passed from one young man to another about trying "Honey Bea's stinger."

As the years passed, the combo of preaching and Honey Bea's stinger increased their popularity with extra money coming in legitimately and illegitimately. Preacher Chase was still in the dark.

One of the "Heaven on Earth" customers had returned to his neighborhood talking about the wonderful experience he had had with a woman preacher who generously extended what she called spiritual opportunities for a stipend. He said the experience made him feel as though he had found "Heaven on Earth." His Uncle, Jackie "The Cobra" Cousin overheard his nephew. "Where and how can I locate this woman preacher? What's her name?" The nephew looked at him, "She's called Honey Bea. She and her father are holding revival meetings out on Mountain Pass Fair Grounds. You can catch up with her there."

The Cobra went to the service, then met Honey Bea at the rendezvous and made later arrangements to find "Heaven on Earth."

The rest is history. He asked her to become his moll. Sensing a new kind of fascination, she agreed on the spot.

Preacher Chase did not give her his blessings, so she sadly left without them.

Drifting into the club car Honey Bea spotted Shadely. Knowing the Topeka stop wasn't far, she prepared to make her move.

Keeping an eye on Shadely, Reson noticed Honey Bea approaching him. Aware of this attractive middle-aged woman's interest in Shadely, his investigative background told him this situation should be monitored. Keeping his distance, he was inconspicuous.

Honey Bea luckily found an available seat next to Shadely and politely asked if it was taken. He looked up, surprised to see her, then smiled and said, "It's available."

She sat down, adjusting her skirt to knee level.

"How far you travelin'?"

Not wanting to divulge his destination, he said, "I haven't made up my mind yet, I'll be looking for work." Not wanting too many questions, he changed the subject. "You going to the west coast?"

She responded, "I'm getting off at Topeka. I'm lonesome, looking for a little company?"

Liking what he was hearing, Shadely thought what a bit of luck. "You're in luck, I hoped to join up with someone for a little fun and frolic."

She followed, "Please don't think I'm presumptuous, but I have a compartment where we might have some privacy."

"It sounds ideal, but we haven't even met. Friends call me Shadely."

"I'm Honey Bea. Now that the formalities are taken care of - let's take a walk."

Shadely thought - this is moving mighty fast - I wonder...Oh well, I've heard of some interesting events on trains. This is one of those opportunities that seldom comes along, he thought to himself. Just take it and enjoy. With that decided, he followed her to her compartment.

Once in, Shadely pulled his tie down to half mast when Honey Bea said, "Just relax, Darlin', I have to run to the little girls' room. Be back in a jiff."

No sooner had she left the compartment than The Cobra barged in. He quickly drew his knife starting for Shadely.

Shadely thought quickly, what was to be a great old time was turning into a nightmare. Deciding to kick at the knife, he screamed, taking The Cobra by surprise. Reson came through the door quickly, hearing Shadely, taking a flying tackle at The Cobra. They went down in a mixture of arms and legs. Blood spurted out of Reson's shoulder where the Cobra stabbed him. Shadely quickly joined the fracas, stepping on the Cobra's hand holding the knife. The knife dropped. Reson grabbed his handcuffs and had the Cobra neutralized in no time. Reson, who'd been watching Shadely, saw the situation develop. When he barged into the compartment, the Cobra was taken completely by surprise. Reson deposited the Cobra in a security compartment where he would stay with him until the train arrived at Topeka. There he would turn him over to the authorities.

While Reson insisted he only did his job, the passengers considered him a hero.

Honey Bea was found hiding in the ladies room where she was taken into custody for being an accessory to the attempted murder.

Reson remained in Topeka to fill out his report. Shadely was permitted to stay aboard, providing he was available for hearings as required.

Visiting with Shadely in the club car, Kit questioned, "How did Honey Bea get you to the compartment so quickly?"

"Well, first of all, I'm susceptible to sexual temptation; secondly, she is attractive; and thirdly, she convinced me she was willing to exchange a few sexual favors. In that I was suckered, it's a blessing that Robert Reson kept a watchful eye on the situation as it developed and then burst into the compartment and helped subdue The Cobra."

Kit followed with, "It's true then that the syndicate sent The Cobra. Have you known him?"

"I've never seen him before and no one has said positively that they did. However, I feel certain it was the syndicate. Who else would have reason to kill me?"

"I don't know. You'd best look over your shoulder. You may be out of markers with the Almighty. Perhaps our paths will cross in

California." Kit stood and returned to his compartment to organize his belongings.

The remainder of the trip to San Francisco was uneventful by comparison.

Kit changed trains in Frisco and traveled on to the village of Tahoe Vista on beautiful Lake Tahoe. The army proving grounds were called Tahoe Sands, Kit's new camp.

His orders specified that he report to the C.O., a Major Strome, head of the bomb testing development team.

Chapter XXXVII

Major Strome was a career man with seventeen years of service. Tall and ramrod straight with rugged, handsome looks, he was every bit army. Rumor had it that while tough as elephant skin, he carried a compassionate heart.

Strome took Kit to his quarters, a small, detached bungalow, housing two officers. The camp billeted six officers in three bungalows and thirty-six enlisted men in six semi-detached cabins, built in 1932 when the U.S. Army acquired the site. The campsite was bordered by the shore of Lake Tahoe at one end and the mess hall at the other, fronting on Lake Drive.

Strome introduced Kit's roommate to him. Pete Ranna was a young, second lieutenant reserve officer in his second year of law at Tulane. A graduate of the Citadel, his home was a small town outside Chester: Ridley Park.

Pete asked, "Tell me, Kit, how'd you manage to get this Tahoe duty?"

"I have a penchant for ordnance, specifically munitions. I requested it and it turned out to be a bombing practice range on this unbelievable lake in the basin between the Sierra Nevada range."

Pete asked, "Where'd you go to school?"

"WMA. How about you?" Kit continued unpacking his duffle bag.

"Citadel. I went there because my Dad thought it would discipline me. It did, but the unexpected happened. I loved the military - the drill, the camaraderie, the rugged life. We're fortunate to be here in one of the most beautiful spots in the States. If I hadn't gone to a military school, I'd have never gotten here. First, my parents sent me to William and Mary. I almost flunked out at the end of the first semester. If I had stayed, I would have. As it turned out, my father pulled me out of the school and made one comment, 'Son you're going to the Citadel; get you some discipline.' It turned out to be the best move he could have made. The school has a great tradition; it did wonders for me."

Kit glanced at Pete, "You know, I never thought about going anywhere but WMA. My Dad wanted to go there but had no money. But it was all he talked about; he influenced me from infancy and when it came time for me, there was no other consideration."

The day passed quickly. Someone suggested a swim in the cold lake. Kit and Pete went in and marveled at the crystle pure water. After a short swim, the water chill forced them out.

After evening mess, the officers sat around a fire on the beach. Those stationed at Tahoe Vista longer, passed along the fascinating tales of Lake Tahoe.

Legend had it that the Washoe tribe came to the lake in the summer as a spiritual place, calling it "Big Water" and "Heavenly Lake." It was higher than any lake in the United States. The Washoe fished and collected grasshoppers which they roasted over hot coals.

The Truckee River fed the 22-mile long lake which became a haven for the affluent from San Francisco around the turn of the century. Several hotels, the Tahoe Sands, the Hotel Bellevue on Sugar Pine Point and the Grand Central Hotel in Tahoe City sprang up accommodating the vacationers that came in the summer.

After the morning drills, Major Strome briefed the new personnel. "Our mission is to run tests on a new weapon called the bazooka. The site here is vast and undeveloped, making it ideal for the purpose of our mission.

"The bazooka, named after and looking like the musical horn invented by Bob Burns, has just been developed and requires refinement through testing. It was developed as an offensive weapon to pierce armor, namely, enemy tanks. In the early development, it had so much recoil action, the kick after firing bruised and battered the soldier's shoulder. Aimed like a rifle, it is a long tube-like weapon that rests on the soldier's shoulder extending in back as well as in front of the shoulder. As the recoil action was corrected, the accuracy of the delivery of the projectile went amiss. The technicians believe they've ironed out the wrinkle. Our job is to make sure the missile hits the target.

"Are there any questions?"

Kit was waiting with his question, "What will our targets be?"

"Our targets will simulate the armor of the U.S.Tank and in some cases the actual tank."

Pete raised his head and caught Strome's eye, "How much damage will the bazooka do?"

"It has been designed to knock out a tank within a given distance. If we can advise the Pentagon that it's firing on target, our mission will be accomplished. If there are no other questions - Dismissed."

The Berman family camped a different spot each summer. Last year Ted Berman, his wife Sonya, and two children Bobby and Laila camped the Yellowstone area in Idaho. This year they chose the wilds of North Tahoe.

Ted Berman was a buck sergeant in a tank crew in World War I. He proudly told his son about his war stories, the battle of Verdun: a prolonged struggle against the Germans.

It was coincidental that the activities at the Vista Sands bomb testing site were occurring at the same time of the Berman's camping visit. Berman discovered the site during a family hike along the northern shore of the lake. The base was protected by a six-foot, chain-link fence topped by barbed wire. "Trespassing Forbidden" signs were everywhere with "U.S.Army Bomb Testing" signs intermittently posted. Naturally, they peaked the interest of Berman. He would inquire about the activities and possibility of civilian tours of the base.

Berman sought his wife's attention, "We have to pick up some steaks for supper. The kids are tired of fish. You know I could eat the mackinaw trout for every meal, but we can pick up our food and supplies in Tahoe Vista."

Berman went into the general store. It was owned by an Indian family. An old Washoe Indian was behind the counter, his dark skin lined deeply from long days in the sun. Greeting Berman with a twinkle in his eye, "How." He smiled, "You new in these parts?"

"Yes. I came for supplies and to inquire about the bomb testing camp."

The Indian helped Berman with his supplies, then said, "I am called Black Hawk. What do you want to know about the base?"

"For starters my name is Berman. I was in the army - army operations interest me. What sort of testing do they do at the base?"

"They test something called a bazooka. It's reported it can stop a tank."

Berman's interest was aroused, "I was in tanks in the army. Bitten by the bug, I'm fascinated with tanks. Do they let civilians on the base?"

Black Hawk looked at him with his interesting black eyes, "They have open house on Wednesday afternoon. No weapon firing, but they go through maneuvers. There are two older tanks that were shipped in recently. I'm told they will be used in the maneuvers on Wednesday.

"Have you any kids?" Black Hawk asked placing the food in a brown bag.

"We have a boy ten and girl four. They love it here. It'll be great for the boy to see the tanks."

On the way back to camp, Berman told his family of the base activities that were open to the public.

On Tuesday morning, Major Strome had his troops prepared for intensive bazooka practice. The metal plates simulating tank armor were the targets.

Kit was one of ten men chosen from both enlisted and officer ranks to fire the weapon. Waiting his turn, positioned to let it rip, his practice included five shots. Kit fired his rounds, each slamming the appropriate mark, proving the required accuracy. As the others went through their exercise, the same results were recorded.

After the drill, Strome rounded up his men. "Our exercises show we are ready to open fire on a tank. Tomorrow, when we have open house, we can practice our tank maneuvers for the actual test on Thursday. The remote controls are working. Lieutenant Ranna, you will be in charge of tank operations. Fox, you and your team, Durning, Dannaker and Simmons will be responsible for weapon testing."

Ranna raised his hand, "I tried the remote controls once. There's been no change?"

"Just the same."

On Wednesday, the Bermans entered Tahoe Sands shortly after noon. The base was busy with visitors crowded into a taped off area. The Bermans joined the group hoping to be near the activities.

Having problems with the tank, Pete Ranna enlisted the help of two base mechanics. All hope was not lost when the tank coughed, started momentarily, then stalled. Two more tries and it started; ready to go.

Hearing Bobby cry out, Mr. and Mrs. Berman both turned to see him on the ground. They rushed over to find him gripping a twisted ankle. They helped him to his feet, but when he walked he favored the ankle. Having seen a red cross on one of the buildings, Ted asked Sonya to take Bobby to the dispensary to be checked while he stayed with Liala.

Liala, being only four, had curly brown hair and brown eyes. She was shorter than most of the crowd. Ted began scanning the crowd but couldn't spot her at quick glance. Looking more closely, he called her name, but his voice competed with the din of the crowd. A woman next to him saw the concerned look on his face and asked, "Who's missing?"

Hearing her question, he looked at her, "My four-year-old daughter."

"What's she look like?"

Still searching the crowd, Ted described her and said she'd only been gone a few minutes.

"I'll report it to my husband, he'll get the word out."

Ted looked at her questioning, "Who's your husband?"

"Major Strome," she replied, motioning for him to follow.

Pete put the tank through tests before he paraded it in front of the visitors. It responded well for an old tired-looking sacrificial lamb. It would be bazooka fodder come Thursday.

Satisfied with the performance, he headed the tank for the run down toward the crowd.

Guiding the tank with his remote control, Pete could operate from a distance. But when not in combat conditions, he walked beside it, easily keeping up as it rumbled noisily along.

Liala had wandered off and stood hidden in a high weeded area. Hearing her father calling her name from a distance, she started toward the voice. As she stumbled through the weeds, lost, she began to cry. She fell to the ground and lay there, scared. Several minutes passed before she slowly got up. Again faintly she heard her father's voice above the noise of the crowd and tried to move toward it.

Suddenly emerging from the weeds, she was directly in the path of the tank. Walking on the far side of the tank, Pete's view was obscured.

Major Strome ordered six of his troops to search for Liala, Kit being among them. Luckily Kit was the first to spot her walking away from the tank, but it was moving faster than she was. Kit yelled to Pete,"Stop the tank! Stop the tank!" The tank noise drowned out Kit's voice. Kit saw the tank bearing down on her. She was still crying and stumbling, still too far away from the crowd of visitors to see her. Fifty yards from her, Kit saw that she would be run over if he didn't take some action. He started to sprint toward her, sensing it might be too late. He tried to shift gears, but he was already at full steam. The tank was just about on her when Kit strained over the last few yards then dove at Liala, knocking her out the path of the tank. As he landed, his foot never cleared the path. The tank ran over the end of his foot as he yanked it away.

He knew his foot was injured badly, but his concern for Liala compelled him to crawl over and console her. Within seconds, other members of the search party were at the scene picking up Liala, rushing back to her parents with her. One stayed back questioning Kit, "We saw you crawling to the little girl, are you hurt?"

"My foot got crushed by the tank; I was lucky to be able to yank it out from under the tread." Kit looked down at his torn shoe, "I'm losing blood and my God, the pain is killing me."

The other officer was Lieutenant Bets, a reservist from Tolchester, Maryland. He told Kit to stay put, he'd get help.

Bets caught up with the medic as he came out of the dispensary. He quickly explained the situation, the medic slung his kit over his shoulder and grabbed a stretcher. They ran back to Kit. Pete was with him.

The medic saw that he was going into shock. Rolling Kit over on his back, he elevated his legs, placing them on anything he could find. Then he gave him a shot of morphine and cut the shoe to help to remove it. Easing the sock off, he saw severe damage to at least two toes and maybe three. He cleaned them up, bandaged the foot, and oversaw the careful placing of Kit on the stretcher. Then he and Bets picked it up and took him to the dispensary.

The nearest medical facility was at Truckee some ten miles distance. The medic was making arrangements to have Kit transferred.

Meanwhile, Liala's parents were hugging her, having heard of the close call. Showing their concern for Kit, they were told he was indisposed. They'd see him another time.

Major Strome stood beside Kit, making arrangements for the official transfer from the base to the civilian hospital. He looked down at Kit, "Looks like you're off to Truckee. We'll keep in contact. We'll notify your wife of these developments and where you may be reached."

Chapter XXXVIII

Dr. Corkran had reviewed the x-rays and examined Kit's foot again. He made his decision: "Lieutenant Fox, let me put it this way. The bad news is you're going to lose three toes, the little and the two next to it. The good news is, we can save the foot and you will be able to use it. If you work at it and are lucky, you should get a near normal use."

"How soon will you operate?" Kit questioned.

"Tomorrow at 7 A.M. The operation should run between two and three hours. After, you will be uncomfortable; we will give you something to ease your discomfort."

Kit frowned, "When will I be able to go home?"

"I'm not sure. We would like you to recuperate enough so that we can monitor your early progress. Perhaps a month."

Kit's mind slowly awakened as the ether wore off. His foot was burning up and hurt like the devil.

By the second day after the operation, the pain was still acute but easing off some.

He received a letter from Mary Lou expressing her very deep concern about the amputation and how she wished she were with him. She considered coming out but had been sick in the mornings, and Doctor Albany advised her against the trip. Yes, she was pregnant. She sent her devoted love and would impatiently wait his return.

So thrilled about the baby, Kit momentarily forgot his own problems.

Doctor Corkran was pleased with the recovery to date. Up on crutches, Kit put a little weight on the foot. It had been a week.

He wrote to Mary Lou, expressing his joy over their expected blessing. He detailed the accident, explaining that it would be another two weeks before his discharge. He told her of Doctor Corkran's comfortable bedside manner, his being raised in Media coming out to college at the University of San Francisco and then venturing down to Truckee to practice. The area was perfect for him with Squaw Valley skiing nearby. Kit closed by telling her to take cautious care of herself and that he loved and missed her.

Kit continued to recover each day, progressing by gradually putting more weight on his foot. In several days he would be using a cane and with the exterior healing, Corkran might send him home.

Kit thought he might push his luck; he asked Doctor Corkran if he might take a day or two over at the Tahoe Hotel for rest and recreation before his discharge . Corkran wanted to see how he functioned with a cane before he was released. Otherwise, Corkran thought it a good idea.

What Kit really wanted to do was rent a horse and ride up the trail on the Rubicon Mountain range bordering Tahoe and see what the "Crown Jewel of the Sierra Nevada" looked like from atop the range.

Corkran released him, and when he arrived at Tahoe City, he checked in at the Hotel Bellevue at Sugar Pine Point on the Lake at the base of the Rubicons. The fashionable Bellevue was a three-story structure used by vacationing San Franciscans.

Before long, Kit found a small ranch where he could hire a horse. Still using a cane, the rancher wondered if he could handle the horse. Kit assured him he could.

The rancher offered him a fine looking Paint, saddled and ready to go. Kit mounted the stallion and rode off slowly to the Rubicon trail. He found he was uncomfortable with his bad foot in the stirrup, so he relieved the pain by pulling his foot out of the stirrup, letting it hang till the pain eased, then putting it back.

CHAPTER XXXIX

Fawn was the product of a French mother and a Washoe father. Her father Swift Deer, worked as a lumberjack chopping trees down as they were needed for various needs at the mining camps in Virginia City.

Moving from one lumbering area to another as the trees were thinned out in the Sierra Nevada, he set up camp wherever he worked. When the demand for lumber ceased, he continued to make his camp in the wilds, living off the land, hunting and fishing. He was medium height, raw boned with muscles of steel. A man of few words and a brisk nature, his black hair and piercing brown eyes drew your attention. In his late forties when he took a woman, they lived together but never married.

Lily was his woman. Just a wisp, she was a maid in the Bellevue and met Swift Deer in the Tahoe City Hotel bar on one of his few visits into town. Joining lumberjacks at their favorite watering hole, they drank heavily, got into brawls and tried their luck on most anything that walked.

One summer night, he had just thrown down three fingers of rye. As his head came back down, he saw her reflection in the mirror behind the bar. Shorter and prettier than her friend, she smiled when he turned around to get a better look, he caught her eye, and winked. She smiled.

That was the beginning of a long affair. Continuing to work, she moved to his camp. He lumberjacked when there was work, and when there wasn't he did odd jobs. He preferred to remain at his camp and enjoy the life of his ancestors, fishing, hunting and roaming the wilds.

Getting her fondest wish, Lily became pregnant. While Swift Deer was now in his fifties, he was inwardly proud, knowing he would have an heir.

He looked at Lily as she grew with her baby, "Old medicine man said squaw with big belly in for big surprise."

"Swift, I feel it will be a girl. If it is a boy, yes, I'll be surprised."

"I'm making a crib for sound sleep and good dreams."

"I wish you'd build a cabin for us so we wouldn't have to go south in the winter."

"Ah, I'd like to, but I don't own the land. We'll migrate south in late summer and return in late spring. Our papoose will learn this custom as I did."

Lily went into labor: long, hard and debilitating. She pushed and cried. The pain was unbearable. She cried out.

Swift Deer inwardly was desperately worried. He held her hand, softly saying, "Breathe deeply, keep pushing, the baby will come."

"I can't do any more than I am. I'm totally spent and weak."

The Indians of old gave birth in the wigwam, managing quite well, delivering in the open fields at times with the help of a squaw or alone. These being the only ways Swift Deer knew, he expected Lily to handle it.

After many, many hours Lily cried out, "The baby won't come out, you'll have to help. Try to find the head and gently pull."

He looked for the baby and saw the head had started to emerge, but it was stuck. If he didn't do something, he might lose them both.

Swift Deer told her he could see the head; he tried to ease the baby out. After another hour, in spite of all the problems, the little girl was born. Because of the peculiar delivery, the baby's head was elongated. The struggle had taken its toll. Swift deer snipped the umbilical court, tying it off as best he could.

Still bleeding, she was exhausted and weak.

She said, "I feel terrible, like I am going to pass out. I don't feel right, I'm scared."

"Lily, just relax, you'll feel better."

"It's not working, I'm bleeding. I just want to sleep."

With that, Lily fell into a deep sleep from which she never awakened.

Swift Deer raised Fawn on the frontier: camping, fishing, teaching her Washoe customs. She learned to fish, hunt, chop wood and cook.

At seventeen, she was beautiful, dark eyes, black hair, a stunning figure. Her awkward birth impaired her advance learning process, however, first impressions and appearances revealed nothing to indicate this disability.

Fawn loved the wilderness, having an affinity toward animal preservation. To this end, she always had an injured finch, rabbit or skunk being nursed back to health so it could take its place back in its natural environment. With the help of her tender, loving nature, her healing intuition enabled her to almost miraculously snatch these animals from the clutches of death and return them to their well being. Sometimes they became domesticated by her caring efforts. Putting them back in their natural environment was delayed many times as they followed her around discreetly, and in turn, she became attached to them.

Kit started up the trail on the Rubicon range that, as legend had it, Kit Carson blazed. It was a beautiful journey with a glancing view of the "Crown Jewel of the Sierra Nevada."

As he had removed his foot from the stirrup to relieve the ache, a deer bolted across the trail, not six feet in front of them. The Paint shied suddenly throwing Kit off, first banging into a tree before falling to the ground with a hard thud, hitting his head on a large rock. He lay on the ground in an awkward position, knocked out cold.

Lingering over Kit for a moment, the Paint then did the expected, and trotted down the trail to the barn.

Fawn was searching for helpless birds or animals along the Rubicon trail several miles from camp. In the distance, she saw something on the ground. Dismounting, she moved up cautiously on foot, not knowing what to expect. Whatever it was didn't move. She thought perhaps it was dead. As she got closer, she could see it was a person, lying very still in an awkward position. After several more cautious steps, she saw it was a man. Noticing he was breathing, she sat beside him. Her helpful nature took over, wanting to help or heal in whatever way she could. As she looked from his chest to his face, she wondered what accident could have occurred out here to render this handsome young man unconscious.

She stayed at Kit's side for another hour or so, not seeing any change in his condition. Instinctively, she felt the need to get him back to camp where she could minister to him.

She rode back to camp for the handmade stretcher, rigged to be pulled by a horse. She returned to Kit where she tugged and pulled, managing finally to move him onto the stretcher. She then began the slow, careful trip back to her camp. There, she was able to drag him into the wigwam where she put him on a deer skin and covered him with her treasured blanket her mother brought with her from Paris.

She missed her father more than ever during times like these wishing he were here to help with determining the injuries the young man suffered. Swift Deer had expired two years ago leaving Fawn to fend for herself. Frankly, she had done quite well. She never missed other people when he was alive, being content with nature and her animals. Lately, though, a strange feeling of loneliness overcame her occasionally. The animals weren't enough so maybe her new ward would fill those gaps of loneliness.

As the hours wore on, she left him alone only to take care of bare necessities. She fetched firewood and started a fire in the late afternoon. She cooked some herbs and fried a trout for supper. Glancing over at Kit as she finished, she noticed his eyes flutter and then open in a squint. Moving over to him, she asked how he felt.

Kit looked at her startled, replying, "I have a horrible headache. Where am I?"

"You are in the Rubicons. Who are you?"

He thought silently, his brow wrinkled, "I don't know. How'd I get here?"

"You were lying by the trail, unconscious when I came across you. I brought you back to camp. You were unconscious for hours with me, before that I don't know. Do you know how you got to the Rubicon trail?"

"Strangely enough, I don't know. I don't remember anything before I awakened here. Is there a town nearby?"

"Tahoe City is several miles from camp. I seldom go there unless I sell some Indian jewelry I have created. Sometimes there are things I need. Once in a great while I trade jewelry or animal skins I cured. Frankly, I don't cotton up to folks. My father said I was shy," she looked down then back up at him. "Would you like something to eat?"

"Yes, I'd like that. I am becoming starved."

After filling up on Fawn's hospitality, a weariness set in and he fell asleep.

She sat by the fire most of the night, thinking about what a handsome, nice, young man he was. She began thinking how she could make him stay. Surely, they would come looking for him.

Fawn didn't have the answer, but she'd ponder the situation, trying to prepare for the inevitable.

Chapter XXXX

After a night of deliberation, Fawn decided her best move to assure keeping her ward would be to break camp before they came looking. Noticing Kit's limp, Fawn imagined it was caused when he hurt his head. As it persisted, Fawn asked why he was favoring his foot. He simply said it was sore. When she asked to see it, they both looked together at the raw spot where the toes were missing. She asked how it happened, but he didn't know and it didn't trigger his memory.

Fawn decided to call Kit "Den," short for dense because he couldn't remember his name or anything else for that matter.

She told Kit she went over to Mount Rose this time of year. Explaining that she would like to help him cure his amnesia, she asked that he go with her. He could ride the horse while she walked. He could see no reason not to make the journey as he had no idea where else he could go.

Mount Rose was to the east of Lake Tahoe, perhaps a two-day journey. She said they would camp at Little Washoe Lake where she camped many times with Swift Deer. Knowing the area was scarcely traveled, Fawn doubted they would be discovered.

When his Paint returned without a rider, the rancher grew concerned. Because of some urgent chores, he was unable to ride out looking until the morrow.

He started out early in the morning not sure which trail Kit had taken. His search turned out to be futile. So he reported the incident to the sheriff's office the next day.

Dr. Corkran was upset when Kit failed to return to the hospital. Telling his assistant to take over, he drove down to Tahoe City. Upon inquiring at the hotel, he learned Kit checked in, went out two days ago and never came back to check out.

His next stop was at the sheriff's office. He was told what they knew, that Kit rented a horse who returned without him. The search party they sent out came up empty.

Corkran contacted Captain Strome at the Tahoe Sands camp advising him of the mysterious disappearance. Knowing more about the situation, he volunteered to call Kit's wife. Strome agreed.

When Corkran phoned Mary Lou, his voice revealed his concern.

"My dear Mrs. Fox, as far as we know, we believe your husband is alive. However, through some strange occurrence, he has disappeared."

She cried, "What do you mean disappeared? When, how, where? It's not possible."

"Mrs. Fox,I share your concern."

He related to her the series of events leading up to the disappearance.

He then followed with, "The local authorities believe he rode into the Rubicon Mountains, but they've been unable to find a trace of him. Captain Strome is arranging another search party of men and officers to look for him."

Sobbing, trying to regain her composure, she spoke as best she could, "I'll tell Kit's mother and father. Please keep me advised of any developments."

"By all means. Rest assured we will press on in our efforts to find him."

Fawn and Kit started their journey taking the Tahoe Rim Trail around the northern end of the Lake. Travel was slow with Fawn walking and Kit's riding inhibited.

As they travelled and spent time together, an unaccustomed feeling overcame Fawn. Den's handsome, rugged looks along with his outgoing personality brought a new unfamiliar feeling to her. The warmth within her, yearned for Den's physical closeness. Bewildered at how to deal with her feelings, she wondered if Den felt the same way.

The trail was rugged, and they rested frequently. Fawn knew all the watering holes where they stopped. Eating off the land, Fawn rustled tasty meals and snacks.

As they grew weary in the early afternoon, they had enough for one day. They set up camp in a tree protected area where a crystal clear stream rambled nearby. Kit was stretched out on a thick carpet of grass when Fawn came over and sat next to him. Thinking long and hard, she decided to take the risk and ask him, "Den, will you kiss me?"

"I've forgotten what it's like, but, yes, I will."

He sat up, leaned over and kissed her on the lips. Their passion stirring, they fell into a longer embrace. Fawn's innocence left her puzzled when he ran his tongue over her lips, working them apart. The sensation released sexual stimulants within her. He broke off the kiss and gave her ear a warm gentle kiss which she responded to by lying down and pulling him with her. His hot breath on her ear and the running of his tongue around the edge down to her lobe, had her catching her breath. She pressed her warm body into his.

Panting lightly she whispered, "Den, please kiss me again."

Kit brought his lips from her ear, turned her head around and looked into her eyes, "Have you been kissed before?"

She held his gaze, "Never like this."

He kissed her again, her lips were parting to welcome his tongue. She touched his with hers, then he ran his tongue around the inside of her lips. Their bodies pressed passionately against each other as their breathing quickened.

Kit's mind raced, he wanted her desperately, to feel her body and more. Subconsciously, a warning feeling arose, making him pull away.

Fawn asked, "Is something wrong? Why did you stop?"

Kit groaned, "I don't know what came over me, but I had this feeling that what we were doing lacked propriety."

"What does propriety mean?"

"It means an acceptable social conduct. For some strange reason, something held me back. Try to bear with my idiosyncrasies."

"What does idiosyncrasies mean?"

"Idiosyncrasies are personal peculiarities."

"I don't think you are peculiar, but perhaps you are not yourself. That blow on your head was a frightful thing. Maybe it made you forgetful."

"My brain was injured at birth making learning by reading difficult. However, I was able to learn many things by observing my father and the few friends he had. He preferred keeping to himself."

"Fawn, whatever problem you have, you certainly hide it well."

"Would you mind if we got something to eat and let things cool down a bit?"

"If you say so. You probably need to rest your foot. Don't you think you could remember what happened to it?"

"I wish I could. I don't remember anything before I met you."

Fawn thought she would like to help him with his memory, but if he regained it, it may mean he would then leave her. Their kissing brought them closer together. She knew little of falling in love.

They ate roasted trout for supper, talked, then settled down for the night.

Early the next morning they broke camp, journeying the last leg to Mount Rose and Little Washoe Lake.

Deciding to abandon the Tahoe Rim Trail, Fawn moved them over to the low trail along the Truckee River. If the hunt was on, it might throw them off their trail. Traveling along the old river was easier as well. Sooner or later, they would pick up an old Indian trail heading south to Little Washoe Lake.

As the sun was starting to set, they came upon the little crystal clear lake, backing up to Mount Rose. Kit marveled at its exquisite beauty. Setting up camp, they supped on dried meat. Weary after the long journey, they bedded down early.

Rain instead of sunshine awakened them. Since their camp was near a cave Fawn had discovered with Swift Deer, they broke camp and ran to it for shelter.

Fawn worked her magic again, producing a fire, lighting up the rear of the cave. They took off their wet outer garments, putting them near the fire to dry. In their underclothes, they stood near it, drying themselves.

In Lima, Gerry left for the Philadelphia train station. Upon his arrival at Lake Tahoe, he planned a search with the cooperation of the troops from the Tahoe Sands Base.

He had visited with Mary Lou, concerned about her well being with Kit missing and her pregnant condition. Actually, she appeared to be prettier than ever, but inwardly she felt the emptiness created by Kit's disappearance. Keeping a stiff upper lip, she assured Gerry she would be fine.

When she asked Gerry what he thought happened to Kit, he told her he could not be prophetic and had no clue as to Kit's whereabouts. He felt, however, that he had the best chance of locating him and that he was confident Kit was fine, being able to take care of himself.

As the train embarked upon its journey west, Gerry was glum about the task at hand.

Fawn made the cave quite homey, hoping it would help when and if a romantic opportunity presented itself. Being clad in their scanty undergarments presented an opportunity for Fawn. She planned an overture which hopefully would send a warming message to Kit.

Going over to where Kit was sitting, she held a pained expression on her face. She had developed a cramp on the inside of her thigh and asked him to massage it away for her. He agreed and put her leg on his. As he massaged, her soft delicate skin distracted him from the task at hand.

Fawn found herself warming and realized the plan might be working. Not having had experienced anything like this before, she was becoming more and more attracted to Kit, but she didn't realize she was falling in love. She did know she didn't want to lose him. In keeping with the plan, she feigned continued discomfort so Kit would keep at it. She positioned herself so their hips were touching. Surprising Kit, she made her next calculated move. She brought her head around so that they were face to face. Then she kissed him gently first, then pushing her tongue through his lips as he had to her. They fell into a heated embrace forgetting about the cramped leg and became overcome by the heated sensations they were experiencing.

Kit gently put his hand on her breast feeling the firm yet soft contours of her virgin body. Removing her bra his lips left hers and went to her breast causing her to catch her breath and then moan softly. The anxiety Kit experienced in their previous encounter was lacking. In the heat of the moment, he removed the rest of her underclothes along with his and rolled over on her. Both were lost in the passion of the preliminaries. Fawn learned very quickly kissing his ears and neck, managing to get all the right spots. Kit eased her legs apart and suddenly Fawn said, "Den, I've never done whatever you are trying to do. I don't know what to do."

"Fawn, you really don't have to do anything. While I can't remember doing it specifically, it's something I feel I've done before. Let's try it together."

Fawn's sexual motor was purring so they proceeded slowly. Suddenly, she felt a sharp pain causing her to cry out softly. Intuitively, Kit knew what had happened. He stopped and asked her if she was okay. She asked for a moment to collect herself, then she'd see. When the pain subsided, she said she was ready to give it another try. They consummated the act with Kit climaxing and Fawn wishing she had a similar feeling, but experiencing enough pleasure to know she wanted to try again.

By now their clothes were dry, they dressed and sat ready to talk a bit.

Kit started, "I'm in a strange state. I don't know who I am or where I'm from. I know nothing about myself."

"Den, if you'll be patient it'll probably come back to you. Meanwhile, why don't we just enjoy what we have?"

"I keep feeling I'm only half a person. I know I'm repeating myself, but I know nothing about anything before I met you."

Fawn feared Kit might venture into town to get some answers. She got him away from Tahoe City and now the nearest was Virginia City, still a distance. Kit didn't remember he was at Tahoe City, Sugar Pine Point and the Bellevue Hotel before he was injured. How? - Fawn might have had some idea, but she was mum.

Kit and Fawn were great companions. They made love, fished and hunted. But it was more than companionship with Fawn, it was love. With Kit, love was forcing itself into his emotions and he was becoming attached to their relationship.

Gerry's trip to the Sierra Nevada took the better part of five days. Captain Strome warmly greeted him when he arrived at the Tahoe Sands Base. Four men were assigned to Gerry to help in the search.

They learned from Dr. Corkran that Kit was headed to Tahoe City. From there they checked all the hotels eventually inquiring at the Bellevue. Gerry checked the desk where he learned that Kit had registered there but hadn't been seen after his registration. Remembering Kit used a cane, the clerk concluded he certainly couldn't walk far.

Gerry thought about the possibilities. In that Kit had no car perhaps he'd found a horse. Asking where horse rentals were available, Gerry was advised of the closest ranch handling horse rentals.

The rancher knew who they were looking for. He told Gerry the Paint his son rented came back by himself. Looking around for signs of Kit, Gerry spotted a cane and asked, "Who uses the cane?"

The rancher replied, "Your son. He left it here when he rode off."

"Do you have any idea where he went?"

"No. Except he rode off into the Rubicons. His bad foot was out of the stirrup, hanging loose. I though maybe he got thrown. Some of us went up the trail looking for him but to no avail. He disappeared mysteriously."

Gerry and the troops started their search, spreading out along the Rubicon Trail. A day's search produced very little. When they returned to the Bellevue, in a conversation with some of the locals, Gerry told them, "We came across what appeared to be some kind of abandoned camp site."

An oldtimer offered, "That was probably the daughter of an old Indian called Swift Deer. They camped in the Sierra Nevadas in the warm months and migrated south in the winter. Her name is Fawn. She's said to be a little touched in the head. You'd never know it to look at her. She's very pretty and acts quite normal."

Thinking a little about what he said, Gerry didn't think it was going anywhere, but he tucked it in the back of his mind.

Back in Chester, Mary Lou was mentally and physically drained. She'd decided to move back into her parent's home until Kit was found and came home.

What nagged at her most was, was he injured? Could he get help? Was he alive? Where was he? All these questions remained unanswered. She felt her place was to be out at Tahoe helping with the hunt. Unfortunately, her doctor had ordered her to rest because her pregnancy was delicate. Normally, calm and serene, she was now impatient, knowing there was nothing she could do but wait to hear from Gerry.

Several weeks passed, Kit and Fawn were getting along just fine. Their camp was in a secluded area near Little Washoe Lake. Just a short distance from camp it opened up to a breathtaking view of the Tahoe Lake and mountains. His memory had not improved.

Unaware of his love for Mary Lou, Kit enjoyed Fawn's passionate liberties. She quickly learned of Kit's pleasure points and enjoyed pleasing him.

At the same time, she was preoccupied with discovering her own sexual pleasures, discarding her inhibitions, deciding that any time and anywhere would be appropriate.

One morning when riding the horse bareback, she turned around and faced him. Her legs went over his and her body was facing his. She smiled at him and said, "Now."

He knew what she meant but kidded along, "Now, what?"

She replied "Fookee."

He laughed at the way she pronounced it. "The horse would be rough on our bottoms and everything else if we stripped below the belt."

Fawn would not be denied. Riding facing each other she could see he was aroused. She pulled up her deer skin skirt and she was ready. "Come on, Den, let's try it."

Kit was still laughing, "I'm sure it would be a first. I frankly can't remember anyone making love on a horse. But then, I'm not remembering anything."

Before he knew what was happening, she unbuttoned his pants and moved so she not only rode the horse but Kit as well.

The horse, confused by Fawn's reverse position and the strange movements, became frisky.

Kit grunted, "Damn, this is a rough ride."

She panted, "It is different. You're enjoying it, aren't you?"

"I wouldn't know, I haven't had time to think about it. I'm busy trying to keep us upright."

Suddenly, the horse gave a buck. Fawn went off one side and Kit off the other. Kit got up, fumbling as he quickly tried to get his flies buttoned. Fawn called out to him in her Indian way, "Our damn horse got kooky and broke up our fooky. But we gave it a good effort."

Kit went over to her as she sat up, "Are you all right?"

"I'm fine, just a little shaken. I suppose if we are going to ride back to camp we should both face the same direction."

Four months had passed since Kit had been injured. He had grown a beard which was a handsome addition to his good looks. Their hygiene necessities were taken care of in the beautifully pure Little Washoe Lake.

In two of the months, Gerry searched the Rubicon Trail area, to no avail. No one reported sighting Kit, and no one knew he and Fawn were together. Gerry had affairs back home which required his attention. Assured that other searches would continue with some regularity, Gerry reluctantly started for home. His plan was to return as soon as possible.

With the constant, close relationship with Fawn, Kit found himself falling in love. He looked forward to the arrival of each day as each one was a new adventure. Each night was filled with passionate love making and sound sleeping brought on by the busy activities of the day. Their relationship became more binding with each passing hour.

In Chester, Mary Lou was trying to deal with her frustrations. Gerry reported seeing no sign of Kit in all his searching. He told her the horse he rented had returned to the ranch. He figured maybe he was uncomfortable riding and dismounted to get some relief. Whatever happened, someone must have helped him because he couldn't travel far. What stumped him was, why hadn't he made some kind of contact with someone? All this uncertainty added to her frustration. Not knowing where her one and only love was and being vulnerable with pregnancy; she wanted and needed him. Remembering her loyal Kit, she felt sure he needed her.

Chapter XXXXI

Kit told Fawn he was taking an early morning ride down to Little Washoe Lake for a bath. As he rode down the trail, a familiar feeling came over him. It was as though he had ridden in a similar surrounding before. As he rode on, the picture in his mind became more clear. In his mind, he was riding the old cavalry trail at White Mountain just north of WMA. WMA! Was his memory coming back? His thought process then went from riding to WMA and now to Win. His next thought was Mary Lou. Suddenly, his mind cleared. It all came back. Mary Lou, my God they were married! What kind of situation had he created? Fawn and Mary Lou; he loved them both. He had to contact Mary Lou.

Shaken, Kit immediately rode back to camp. Fawn was surprised to see him so soon.

Kit called over, "Fawn, I've got my memory back!"

"When did it happen?" She had no animation in her voice.

"It happened as I was riding down the trail toward the lake." He explained how his memory started to return.

They sat down facing each other. The images came flooding back to him.

Kit started, "I'm in the army reserve and I was sent to Tahoe for my two weeks duty. I injured my foot in an accident. I came to the Rubicons on a weekend to recuperate. I hired a horse and got thrown hitting my head. I lost my memory. The rest you know."

"What happens now?" She asked reluctantly.

"Honey, there is no easy way to tell you this. I'm married. My wife's name is Mary Lou. I must call her. She must be a wreck, and she's also pregnant. I'll also have to see the doctor who operated on me and then contact the base at Tahoe Sands."

"What'll happen to us?" she asked sadly, tears in her eyes.

"God knows. I love you and I love Mary Lou. Legally and morally I belong with Mary Lou. I know what's right, but I've terribly mixed emotions. I know I must call her as soon as possible."

"Den, I don't want to lose you. I love you and I'll take care of you. Why don't we give it more time?" She was grabbing at straws.

"I must get to town and make some calls; my family wonders what happened to me."

"Why can't you forget the calls? By now, they must figure you're dead; we could just go on as we have. It would be wonderful," trying to sound cheerful but afraid her words were in vain.

"As much as I'd consider it, I can't. I must make those calls. It's better if we break camp now and get on the trail."

"Den, damn it, I don't want to go. I'll have nothing if you leave. It's not fair to me. I've never known love like this. I love you with all my heart," her words pleaded as her heart grew heavier.

"Fawn, my name is Kit. Kit Fox. I've been happily married, and I'm going to have a baby. This situation we find ourselves in wasn't planned, it just came about. Neither of us is responsible. It's going to be difficult, but I know absolutely what I am going to do. I'm going home to my family. Your taking up with me had its risks."

"I'm going to continue to call you Den. Yes, I know there were risks. That's why we travelled over here to Mount Rose, so no one would find you. I did it on purpose - I didn't want to lose you. The longer we were together, the more my love grew. I'd hoped yours would've grown likewise and you would've preferred to remain rather than return to whatever."

"Fawn, I can't in good conscience delay my contacting Mary Lou and returning to her. I'm going to start breaking camp. We can travel back to the Bellevue together. Maybe you could open your camp back there."

"I'll kill myself, if I lose you," she threatened.

"Don't talk that way, it'll all work out."

"Cut it out, Den! It'll be okay for you, but not me. Without you, I have nothing. You taught me how to make love, you taught me how to love. Without you, I'll die," her words had a cutting sharpness.

"You are being impetuous. Things are difficult,but time is a panacea. Certainly,you got along before you met me. You're making it so much more difficult for me. If I didn't love you, I'd simply walk away. I'm torn between you and Mary Lou. My rightful place is with her and my unborn child. Sorry, I guess I'm repeating myself. I'll do anything I can to help you short of staying here. Try to rationalize things this way: you're facing a trying situation, however, you've got youth and beauty in your favor. If you give yourself a chance, things will work out for you."

She rushed into his arms, sobbing her heart out, unable to talk. Kit held her tightly while she sobbed.

"Come on, Fawn; we'll travel back to the Bellevue where you can drop me off. Then you can go back to your camp in the Rubicons. Meanwhile, I'll make every effort to find you employment if you would like me to."

Fawn slowly stopped crying and reluctantly agreed. The trip was noticeably strained as Fawn was chagrined and said nothing except an occasional answer to Kit's attempts to ease her pain.

As they approached the Bellevue, she asked that he dismount. She had walked while he rode. As he got off the horse, she made her plea.

"Kit, I like your name - you know, we could be so happy together. You have all my love and I know you love me."

Kit looked at her and thought how beautiful she was, how thoughtful and caring for anything that needed help. She indeed was a remarkable young lady. He knew he had to make the break quickly as it was becoming more and more difficult. "I'm sorry Fawn, what you say is true, but I'm going to leave you now. If I don't, I may not be able to." He walked away slowly, trying not to look back. After a minute or so, he turned to take one last look. She was sitting on her horse with tears streaming down her cheeks. He gave her a half-hearted wave then continued to walk away, hiding his own choked-up emotions.

As he approached the Bellevue, several of the soldiers assigned to the hunt spotted him, naturally assuming it was he. Their inquiry proved correct. He immediately went to a phone to call Mary Lou. When he got through and told her he was fine, she burst into tears of joy. After she composed herself, she asked why he hadn't called her sooner. He explained his riding accident and how he had lost his memory. He was deep in the Sierra Nevada when he recovered it, just two days ago. It had taken him that long to get back to town, and then he called her immediately. The story, being as complicated as it was, would be better explained in person and he told her as much. Ecstatic about his well being, she just wanted to know when he would be home. Kit assured her he would be home after he checked in with Dr. Corkran and his Vista Sands base.

Dr. Corkran examined Kit's foot and to his surprise found it had healed nicely. Dr. Corkran had Kit examined by a neurologist. He diagnosed the head injury as a concussion from which Kit appeared to have recovered. Kit got his release and returned to Vista Sands, but not before he told his tale.

Major Strome met Kit when he arrived at the base.

"Greetings to my wanderlust Lieutenant. I understand you made a tour of the Sierra Nevada. How long did you have amnesia?

"All but the last few days."

"How did you come by the young Indian gal?"

"She found me when I lay unconscious after my Paint threw me. She helped me during my recovery. When we traveled, she let me ride her horse while she walked. With no memory, I didn't know what my past was or where I should have been. As it turned out, Fawn kept us on the move because she liked taking care of me and she didn't want us to be found. When my memory came back, we broke camp and came on in."

Strome responded, "That's quite a story."

"Yes, well, if you can accommodate me, I'd like to return home as soon as possible."

Kit got his orders. His summer tour was complete, and he was to return to inactive reserve status.

Chapter XXXX11

Mary Lou, Phil and Gerry met Kit at the 30th Street Station in Philadelphia. The homecoming was one of laughter and tears, expressing joy and warmth none of them had ever experienced. Kit smiled, observing Mary Lou's bulging belly, and they embraced, hugged and kissed oblivious to the crowds of people moving through the terminal.

When Mary Lou and Kit got home and settled in, she pulled out two T-Bones she purchased for the occasion, mixed up a salad and put two potatoes in the oven. She served the medium rare steaks on a candlelit table. The dinner was superb. After cleaning up the kitchen, Mary Lou brought him a piece of warm apple pie with a dollop of vanilla ice cream piled on top.

Unable to hold back her curiosity, Mary Lou felt it was time to hear about his exploits. "I'm anxious to hear about your time at Tahoe. Why don't we just move into the living room and get comfortable? I forgot to ask how your foot feels, I was so excited to see you."

He began, "You knew about the accident at Tahoe Sands and my trip to see Dr. Corkran in Truckee. After that I was to spend a weekend in the Rubicon area, and I chose the Bellevue Hotel to be my home base. I hired a horse for a ride up the mountain trail. My foot was bothering me so I took it out of the stirrup. Somehow or other I got thrown, and hit my head on a rock. I was knocked unconscious."

"Is that when you lost your memory?"

"Yes. Before I gained consciousness, Fawn, the young Indian maiden, discovered me and took me to her camp."

"Was she pretty?"

Kit answered, "Very. She had some brain damage at childbirth which you can barely determine. She was a great gal. She eventually moved us on, as she didn't want me to be discovered."

"Why didn't she want you to be found?"

Kit continued, "Let me go back a bit. Her mother never recovered from the difficult delivery so she was brought up by her father, a full-blooded Washoe. She had enough schooling to know how to read and write. Because her father was concerned about her condition, she led a very sheltered life. She always loved animals, and as she grew up, she acquired a penchant for taking care of injured animals. After her father died, she spent as much time as possible nursing these animals back to good health. Mostly she lived off the land, but when she found a need for money, she took odd jobs, working around the Bellevue or helping women with their laundry or house cleaning. When she came across me, unconscious, it was her nature to take care of me. When I regained consciousness and we got to know each other a bit, she started to feel attached to me and nursing me back to my normal self became a challenge she intended to meet.

"Having lost my memory, I had no compulsion to leave. Actually I was enjoying myself."

Mary Lou asked, "Being together all the time, with no other people around, could have been conducive to intimacy, couldn't it?"

"Ultimately, yes, it did. In my condition, I had no reason to inhibit my emotions."

Kit realized the chilling effect the truth would have on their relations; however, he justified it knowing it would have never occurred had he not had amnesia. He was always honest with Mary Lou and knew he owed her this story.

"Eventually, we did become emotionally involved. Having been so sheltered, she had no experience, but once we kissed she found she enjoyed it. One thing led to another eventually. But suddenly, I had an inner feeling indicating what I was about to do wasn't right. I didn't know why.

"The next time, she came to me and said, 'I want to kiss.' Before we knew it, nature took its course again. However, this time there was no cautious inner feeling, and we made love. The relationship went on and we fell in love."

Mary Lou choked up, but she made the ultimate effort not to break into tears. She stood up and walked over to look out the window with her back toward Kit. When she felt she could talk, she said, "I'm so happy you're safe and healthy, but this is a bitter pill I never even considered. It's like shell shock. The circumstances are so bizarre, I have a terrible time accepting them. I was home pregnant, worried to death about your survival; and, ironically, you were in the mountains making and falling in love with a young Indian girl!" Her words were filled with anger and uncertainty.

"You're absolutely right; however, as soon as I regained my memory, I ended the romance and returned."

"I may be leaning toward paranoia, so forgive me when I ask, how do I know if you broke it off as soon as your memory returned? The fact that you have always been an honorable, trustworthy person is reassuring. I must admit it'll take an enormous adjustment for me to get back to where we were. It compounds the problem when I think of you making love to someone else."

She hesitated for a time then went on, "Since we have just been separated, this may sound untimely, but I need a little space. I don't know quite how to deal with it. My emotions are in a turmoil. If I go to my parent's home for a few days and try to sift out the uncertainties, perhaps I'll be able to cope."

Kit responded, "I respect your feelings, but I wish you would stay and let me try to help. Now that I'm home, I know it's where I belong...with you. We've built a great relationship, and we should now work harder than ever to preserve it. The incident was very unfortunate but due totally to fate. I'll make it up to you, I promise."

"Do you still love Fawn?"

"Honestly, yes, I do have a feeling of love. But it was like I was in another world for a short period of my life. Given time, I'm certain that the love will pass."

Mary Lou came over to Kit and caught his eye, holding it she said, "I'm sorry, Kit, but I think it's better to leave for a time so that I can try to put my emotional house in order."

Mary Lou left and they agreed that he would give her five days before he came to take her to dinner.

At the Folkner home, Mary Lou talked with her mother, trying to overcome her doubts. Her mother encouraged her to return to Kit, pointing out that he was a fine young man and not responsible for the unfortunate incident.

Mary Lou said, "But Mother, I am having trouble with his loving and making love to that Indian girl."

Mrs. Folkner replied, "Naturally you would, but you need to forgive him, he wasn't himself. Normally, he would never do anything like that. As your life continues, you'll be surprised at the number of spouses who are unfaithful, even by design, but are eventually accepted back by their partners."

"I hear you Mother, I'm not like all those people! I'm not ready to go back and act like everything is normal when it isn't. I can't just say 'okay let's get on with life,' when he fell in love with someone else, and still loves her. Regardless of his amnesia, it's not in the cards. At least, not yet."

"Mary Lou, I can't force you to go back, but remember he is a handsome, gregarious young man whom many young ladies would flirt with in a minute with you not at his side. Look at what happened at Lake Tahoe."

That got her attention. "Mother, I don't have a bellicose feeling toward Kit. I love him. I don't want other aggressive women making passes at him. I don't want to drive us further apart, but I can't help my feelings. I hope I can rationalize. To make the problem go away would be perfect. On the other hand, I don't want him to think I countenance his promiscuity."

Mrs. Folkner decided to drop the topic and get on to something else. Perhaps relieving the concentration on the problem would indirectly help Mary Lou sort out her feelings.

Kit was back at work, his foot healed and he had no further effects from the head injury. The business took his mind off Mary Lou's self imposed separation. When he returned to the apartment, he became obsessed with melancholy. He did very little besides eat and ponder his problem. He felt cheated by the bad hand fate dealt him. It was turning his life upside down, and there was very little he could do about it.

At work, Betty Dud, a recently hired stenographer, heard of Kit's plight and decided to make the best of his situation. She was an attractive, blue-eyed, blond, well endowed with a pleasing personalty. She admired Kit's handsome features and keen mind; she was pleasantly surprised when this opportunity presented itself.

When Kit returned to the shop after a day's work of servicing heaters, Betty confronted him. She explained that the heater in the bungalow she rented was not working properly and asked him to stop by after work and take a look at it. Kit agreed.

Kit knocked on the bungalow front door. Betty answered with "Come in, Kit. May I get you a drink?"

"No, thanks. Would you show me where your furnace is? I'll check it out. Do you have a service policy?"

"Not yet. I only moved in two weeks ago. Follow me, I'll show you to the cellar." She walked out of the living room down the hallway to the cellar steps. Walking down the steps, Kit went over to the heater.

"What's the problem?"

"When I push the thermostat, the heater doesn't go on."

The first thing Kit checked was the gauge in the oil tank. It was on empty.

"Betty, you're out of oil. We can call for a delivery. The delivery man may have to prime the motor. Be sure you tell him you ran out of oil."

Betty made the call then turned to Kit, "Is it true that you are footloose and fancy free?"

"Not exactly, I'm married."

"I noticed you didn't say 'happily'."

Kit turned away uneasily. He didn't answer.

"I was told your wife left you."

"It's only a temporary arrangement. She'll be back soon."

"Would you like to stay for supper? I can put in a meatloaf quickly. How about it?"

"Thank you for your thoughtfulness, but I'm going to run along. See you at the shop in the morning."

"Tell me something, Kit. Have you ever thought of cheating on your wife?"

"Not under normal circumstances."

"I'm available if you decide you might want to give it a try."

"Thanks again, but I'm still a married man."

Betty said, "We could make passionate love together. I guarantee it. How about a kiss."

"I'm sorry, Betty, I'm leaving."

As Kit walked down the front walk, Betty stood in the doorway watching him. A car drove slowly by the front of the house.

When Kit took Mary Lou out for their scheduled date, they went to dinner at the Clover Leaf Inn for some of the their famous pasta. The restaurant and bar were in the converted basement of the family home. As you walked in, you were greeted by the friendly ambience and tempting aroma of tomato sauce cooking in the kitchen. They chatted with a few friends they met as they arrived, before edging over to a secluded booth.

After settling in, they both ordered draft beer and an order of spaghetti and meat balls until their waiter, Wilbur, told them they had home-made ravioli. Mary Lou changed her order. Lingering over their beer, waiting for their dinner, Kit's thoughts drifted back to the situation Betty had created, and how he yearned for his relationship with Mary Lou to be back to normal. In any event, he wasn't going to discuss that issue. He caught her eye, "How close are we to becoming a family again? I'm miserable with this separation and I'm anxious to join together and enjoy the many blessings our marriage should be creating. I do really love and miss you."

Mary Lou reached for his hand and held it, "I love you and hope my uncertainty will pass quickly. I'm making progress. Please have patience with me."

"I will, but it's not easy."

Their dinners came and they dined, enjoying every mouthful. Their conversation became more casual as they downed several more beers.

After the short drive home, they sat in the car. He was uncertain how she would react to an advance. Finally, he put his arm around her shoulders and pulled her over to him. He kissed her and she responded passionately, having been celibate since he had left for Tahoe. As he reached down and cupped her breast, Mary Lou suddenly thought of Kit cupping Fawn's breast and she pulled away. "This could easily lead to passionate love making."

Kit countered, "That's what I'm hoping."

Mary Lou looked at him seriously, "I'm sorry, but I'm not ready yet."

Kit kissed her lightly on the lips, then said, "That's not what I was hoping to hear, but I respect your feelings. It seems we may be making some progress. I loved being with you. I suppose we should call it an evening. Will you call me if you have a change of heart? I'll drop whatever I'm doing and rush to you immediately."

Mary Lou smiled, "Yes, I will. As much as I hate to see you go, you better before my inhibitions desert me."

Kit walked Mary Lou to the door where they said good night.

The next day Kit went to Stackeys, a new hoagie shop, to try their fare. He was enjoying the wondrous taste of the blend of ham, salami, provolone, onions, tomatoes and olive oil on a fresh baked Italian roll when in walked Betty. She ordered her Italian delight, came over to Kit's table and sat down with a "Hi. Imagine meeting you here."

Kit, through his surprise, said, "Hi. Do you come here often?" What he hoped to do was eat and get the hell out.

She laughed, "Only when I follow you."

After the evening they'd spent together, Mary Lou had decided she was ready for a try at a reconciliation. She drove down to the plant, looking for Kit at lunch time. She went into the office asking for him and was told he was at Stackey's. She got back in her car, drove there, parked and walked toward the hoagie shop. As she approached, she looked through the pane glass window. Kit and

Betty were sitting at the same table, eating and talking. Her paranoia surfacing, she turned away, went back to her car and drove home.

That evening at dinner she explained the Stackey scene to her parents.

Hearing this, her father offered, "Until now, I felt there was no reason to mention this. But the other evening, I was driving home to dinner, and I saw Kit coming out of a house. There was a woman at the door watching him walk away. I simply thought he had been on a service call. But now I wonder."

Mary Lou said, "I'll find out whose house it is if you remember the address."

"Give me a moment and I'll recall it."

Mary Lou checked the address at the municipal building to learn that the house was owned by one James Bomen, an absentee owner from the midwest. He had lived in it until he'd been transferred from the area. Now he kept it as a rental property. She learned the agent handling the rental was a realtor by the name of Andersen. She visited Andersen's office and asked if they could tell her the name of the tenant in the Bomen house. The secretary asked why she wanted to know. Mary Lou told her it was for personal reasons. The secretary said she could not reveal the name arbitrarily without good reason. Mary Lou asked to see Mr. Andersen.

The secretary tried to screen pesky people, however, this girl persisted. She excused herself and went to Mr. Andersen's office. Andersen came out and immediately recognized Mary Lou as a daughter of an old friend. He questioned her briefly then told her the tenant was Betty Dud.

Mary Lou parked a half block from Betty's house early in the morning so she could follow her to find out where she worked. When Betty drove away, Mary Lou followed her at a discreet distance. Betty drove directly to the Fox business where she parked and went in. Mary Lou waited to see if she came out. She didn't.

With this new development, she fell into a deep depression. She told her parents about Betty. Her mother still felt Kit was innocent. She said these incidents could easily be happenstance.

Mary Lou couldn't shake Kit's involvement with Fawn. That, coupled with these new developments, made her reconciliation with Kit difficult if not impossible. She didn't trust herself to talk to him so she sent him a note telling him she would be unable to meet this week as planned, and she would advise him as to their future meetings. She told him not to bother contacting her; she would contact him when she sorted things out.

Kit came home from work to find Mary Lou's note just a day before they were to meet. He decided to respect her edict, but he had to find out why the turn of events.

The next day Kit called Mr. Folkner from the plant. After the usual greetings, he asked, "Sir, I'm concerned about a note I received from Mary Lou. She is cutting off all communications. I thought we were making progress and perhaps we would be able to get back together. Could you at least tell me what the problem is?"

"Kit, I don't know all the details, but she thinks there may be someone else in the picture."

"Sir, that's ridiculous, I love her, I want to be back with her."

"Kit, you can't blame her for having reservations. I personally hope you two can resolve your problems."

"Would you please tell her I love her and hope to resume living together as a family?"

"Kit, I'll convey your message."

When Mary Lou got the message she thought carefully, then said, "That's all well and good, but I don't feel confident about his love. Not too long ago, he told me he still loved Fawn and me. I feel wretched about the whole thing."

Meanwhile, Kit was living his own personal hell. It never entered his mind that Betty was the obstacle. He thought the someone-else-in-the-picture was Fawn. Reflecting, he thought he probably would have been better off if he had lied to her, but that was not his nature. He still had a place in his heart for Fawn; there was no denying that. But he knew his proper place was with Mary Lou; and if he could get on with it, he was sure they would find that time would take care of everything.

He was very busy at work which partly took his mind off the ever-present problem. Unfortunately, Betty continued to encourage an association between them whenever she could. She tried to catch his attention when he arrived or left work or when she could find him at lunch. Annoyed by her confrontations, he took to going to his apartment for lunch. She did finally catch him one night as he was leaving, walking to his car. Startling him, she came around from the rear of his car as he unlocked the driver's side door.

She asked, "Have you been avoiding me?"

Kit looked at her surprised, "As a matter of fact, I'd been hoping we wouldn't meet. I told you I'm married and I'm not interested in you."

"Well, I've been watching you and you don't look very happy. I feel I could help you. Why not give it a go?"

"Sorry, Betty, I've told you I'm not interested. Why don't you beat it?"

"Kit, I know if I persevere, you will eventually break down."

"Don't count on it. I'm taking off. Give me a break and ease off."

"I'm not going to give up. You'll hear from me."

Kit eased into his car and drove home, dejected and frustrated.

Actually, he had more time on his hands with Mary Lou at her parents. He saw Gerry at work every day but didn't want to burden him and Phil with his problems. To pass the time, he often walked over to the college campus.

After he arrived home from his encounter with Betty, he strolled over to the campus. As he approached Old Main, two men came hurrying out the door at the southern end of the Old Main. They saw Kit and stopped dead in their tracks. Kit looked at them and smiled.

"Look at you two, Prof. Johnston and Dean Cole, what a pleasant surprise. You both look like WMA agrees with you.

"I wouldn't be surprised to see either or both of you leave your academic mark on these hallowed halls."

Professor Johston said, "We heard about your activities this summer. How's the foot?"

"The foot's remarkably good. I just wish my personal life was doing as well."

Dean Cole looked at him questioning, "What's happened?"

Kit asked them if they could go over to the Alumni Lodge for a cup of coffee so he could tell them his tale of woe.

After Kit finished, they both looked at one another shaking their heads. Finally Dean Cole said, "I'm afraid this is one time we are unable to advise you. I've got an idea. It's not the answer to your problems, but it might get your mind off it for a time. Why don't you come over to my house for dinner?"

"That's a great idea. I'd appreciate it."

"Well, come on out to the house. Dinner'll be ready by the time we get there."

After a dinner and visit filled with nostalgic conversation, Kit returned to his lonely apartment and went through the mail. Nothing from Mary Lou. He showered and called his folks.

Phil answered.

"Hi, Mom."

"Kit, I've wondered how you are doing. Dad tells me some, but it's not the same as hearing it from you. Have you heard from Mary Lou?"

"No. I wondered if you see her, Mother, and if so, what she may have to say."

"Kit, I've seen her. She wishes you'd get back together."

"I'd like nothing more, but the gap seems to widen. I'll keep trying. We belong together.

"I was thinking about you. I'll stop out soon."

"Kit, please take care of yourself."

"Don't worry, Mom, I will. Love ya. Bye."

Kit read a bit and retired. He'd just fallen asleep when the phone rang. It was Mrs. Folkner, and she told Kit Mary Lou had had a fall. There were indications she might miscarry. They rushed her to Chester Hospital.

Kit thanked her, put his clothes back on and sped to the hospital.

Kit arrived after midnight. He inquired and got her room number. A nurse came out as he approached. She walked up to him and asked if he was Mrs. Fox's husband. Answering affirmatively, he asked if he could see her. She said of course, but she was asleep. He said he'd be quiet.

He simply stood watching her as she slept peacefully. How he wished he could tell her he loved her, hold her in his arms, help her in her time of need. After staying for two hours, he left his phone number with Nurse Ayers, and asked that she call him should there be any changes, then went home.

Kit awoke with a start at quarter to seven. The realization that Mary Lou was in the hospital brought him out of his sleep.

When he left for work, he stopped at the florist for a dozen red roses and went to see Mary Lou on his way. When he got there, he was told she would only see her parents. Depressed, he left the roses and went on to work.

Mary Lou was feeling better when Miss Ayers brought her the roses. She had time to think. Suddenly, a bellicose feeling came over her: she was going to fight for Kit. She loved him and was married to him. But he'd have to wait until she planned her battle attack. As soon as she felt well enough, she'd make her move.

After leaving the hospital, she recuperated at her parents' home. By the end of three weeks, she was feeling fit and decided it was time. She revealed her plan to her parents and immediately got their support. But concerned for her health, they didn't want a repeat of what landed her in the hospital.

She did her homework by observing Betty's movements. She learned she usually arrived home from work around 6:30 P.M. Following further monitoring, at 6:00 P.M. on a Thursday, Mary Lou parked a half-block from Betty's house. At 6:35 Betty pulled up, got out of her car and went into her house.

Mary Lou waited for several minutes, then went and rapped on the front door.

Betty answered, "Yes, may I help you?"

"Yes, I'm Mary Lou Fox. May I come in?"

Betty shifted uneasily, wondering what this visit might bring with it, "What is it you want?"

"I should pull your hair out, but I'll start out requesting a few words."

"It's against my better judgment, but okay, come on in."

Mary Lou went in, Betty showed her a seat in her living room then said, "What's this all about?"

Mary Lou was ready for anything, "Why are you after my husband?"

"Is that all you want? Let me give you some advice. If I were married to Kit, I wouldn't be letting him roam around. I 'd make sure I was home with him keeping him happy. You don't know how lucky you are. He refused every pass I made to seduce him. I planned all my moves. He never sought me out."

Mary Lou was so surprised she was without words for a few moments. Regaining her composure she said, "You've been a great help. I'll be on my way."

Walking back to her car, Mary Lou thought how fortunate she was the confrontation went so smoothly, and actually what a help it was. In her condition, anything more involved might have triggered some sort of relapse.

She started driving toward her parents' home when suddenly she could no longer hide her emotions. She turned toward the apartment driving faster. Walking up to the front door, she could see the lights were on through the windows. Kit was home.

With a look of surprise, he answered the door. "Mary Lou. I can't say I'm not surprised, but I sure am glad to see you. Is this a friendly visit?"

"Yes, it is."

"The last thing I remember...you didn't want to see me. What happened?"

Mary Lou smiled her most alluring smile, "First things first. Can we go inside?"

"Excuse me. Of course. I was just about to rustle up something to eat."

He led her to the kitchen where they each took a seat at the kitchen table.

Mary Lou smiled again, "Do you still want me back?"

"To tell the truth, I thought it was over...your refusing to see me and all."

"After Miss Ayers brought your roses to me, I suddenly realized I wanted you and I would have declared war on whomever I had to, I'd have fought for you."

Kit just listened.

Mary Lou didn't miss a beat, "I just didn't know. I thought you were having a time with that Betty girl in your office." She told him about seeing him with her in Stackey's Hoagie Shop, about her father seeing him leaving Betty's one early evening, and about her confronting Betty. She revealed how helpful Betty's reassuring message regarding Kit's loyalty was. "I know I was stubborn coming around, but I'm ready to live together as a loving family if you are."

"Mary Lou, because you've made me wait these long days, I'm going to leave our reuniting up to chance. I'll flip this coin, heads you stay, tails you go back to your parents' home."

Mary Lou started to protest.

Before she could say anything, Kit flipped the coin, caught it and turned it over on the back of his other hand. He took his hand off the coin, looked at it and said, "Heads it is. Looks like you're staying," and handed her the coin.

Mary Lou looked at it then turned it over. It was a two-headed Indian head nickel.

Epilogue

Four months after their reconciliation, Mary Lou delivered what she and Kit thought was the most beautiful eight-pound little girl ever. She was christened KITTEN Fox.

Fawn always hoped to care for a big animal. She eventually found a big elk.

Fate cast its good fortune on her and she wed a Shoshone-Bannock descendent. A fine, handsome widower from Idaho, he'd settled on a small ranch near Thunder Canyon outside Lava Hot Springs.

It started when she was recovering from her depression after the breakup with Kit. She'd headed north to find the Fort Hall Reservation near Pocotella. After one of many long, tiring days, while passing through Lava Hot Springs, she decided to soak her weary bones in the famous hot mineral springs used by early Native Americans for its remedial magic.

Unbeknownst to her, her future husband simultaneously planned a soak in the soothing springs. He'd just finished a round up at his spread bordering the Portneuf River. Hot and tired, he headed for the springs where he jumped into the lukewarm pond. Sitting in the pond with water up to her neck, Fawn rested, slowly moving her arms and legs, totally relaxed. The splash from his jump soaked her head.

At first surprised, Fawn became indignant as she saw the big man smile when he noticed her soaking head.

The big fellow, still wearing a smile, said, "So sorry, I didn't notice you when I jumped. Then when I did, it was too late. I was in the air."

"You should be more careful. Other people are here besides you," she wiped her eyes with her hands.

Still smiling, he said, "Just your head was out of the water, I guess that's why I didn't notice you. Let me make it up to you, why don't you join me for supper when you finish soaking?"

Fawn thought for a minute. What did she really have to lose? He was handsome, looked Indian, but she'd make it a little difficult. "I don't think so, I don't even know who you are. You're also a smart aleck."

"My ancestors were Shoshone-Bannock. I'm really rather shy, seeing you getting soaked struck me funny. Why not ease up and have some supper with me? We'll go over to the Chuck Wagon. Wonderful grub. What do you say?"

She was beginning to like him. "You've got yourself a date. I'll go change."

They had their supper at the Chuck Wagon and the rest is history... His name was Big Elk.